PRINCE OF
SLOTH

PRINCES OF SIN:
SEVEN DEADLY SINS SERIES

K. ELLE MORRISON

DEAR READERS

This book contains material that may be considered inappropriate for readers under the age of 18.

These materials cover:
Graphic sex between consenting adults.
Depictions of violence. Elements of religious trauma.
Your mental health is important to me, please proceed with caution if any of these things make you feel uncomfortable.

Please leave a review ;)

To anyone who didn't think I could make Sloth sexy…
Bet.

OTHER TITLES BY K. ELLE MORRISON

To stay up-to-date on upcoming titles, bonus material, advanced reader opportunities, and so much more visit Kellemorrison.com to join the newsletter!

For signed paperbacks, new merch, and all upcoming projects and updates from K. Elle Morrison please subscribe to the _FREE_ Newsletter!

For NSFW art, first peeks at up and coming works in progress, and signed paperbacks delivered right to your door check out K. Elle Morrison's Patreon!

Kellemorrison.com
Linktree

It really was him.

Ezra St. Croix. The lead singer of Luci in Furs was sitting in the VIP section of The Deacon.

He was even sexier in person.

I'd seen him in concert once, but that was before the band had gone on hiatus years ago. How could he look younger than he had way back then?

That didn't matter. I needed to get closer to him. Talk to him.

I glanced left, then right. No one gave me a second look as I picked up a tray filled with drinks from the bar. I could pass for a waitress as long as I acted the part. He didn't have security hovering around. The Deacon was exclusive enough that he likely felt safe here without the extra bodies.

I held the drinks above my head as my hips weaved through the dance floor. Adrenaline and the bass from the DJ booth pounded against my eardrums. My friends had ditched me at the door and were grinding on the dudes they'd met at the bar. Neither of them bothered to glance at me as I passed them. I took a deep breath and stepped out of the crowd.

Fuck, he was gorgeous. His black hair was all slicked back except for a few rebellious locks that dangled over his brow and tipped at the top of his cheekbones to frame his crystalline eyes. Smudges of black and red liner around each eye made it impossible to ignore where his irises were wandering. Tattoos crept up his neck and down his exposed arms. I wanted to memorize every single dot of ink with my tongue. I'd read in gossip magazines that he had more than just his nipples pierced, and I wanted to find out for myself. The thought made my mouth water.

Get it together, Pru.

I squared my shoulders and strode over to him, the tray presented to him just below my chest. He smiled up at me.

My insides went to goo.

"Thank you, lovely," he said with a wink. He took one of the shot glasses full of amber liquid from the tray.

I did my best to distribute the weight change in my palm. I'd never forgive myself if I spilled four glasses of booze in his lap.

"Are you new?" he asked, eyeing me. "My brother rarely hires . . . women."

I had no time to dwell on that sexist policy. "I'm just covering a shift for the night."

A lie.

A small one, but by the time he figured it out, we would surely be in love and ready to skip off to Europe for a vacation in Venice.

He knocked back the shot, placed the empty glass on my tray, and lounged back against the large, scooped chair. I glanced around, but he seemed to be alone, or maybe he was waiting for someone.

"You're cute," he said, sending a gush of excitement into my belly. "Don't get mixed up with any of these losers here. I would hate to see them fuck you over."

Was that an opening?

"Maybe I should hang out with you, then?"

His whole face brightened. The curl of his lips made my knees weak. I hadn't entered the club with this much audacity, but I was lucky it had found me.

He stood up, and I took a deep breath as his tall, lean torso ate up my vision. The music and other bodies around us disappeared as he leaned down to whisper in my ear. "I think I'd really enjoy your company. But out of everyone in this club, I would be, by far, the worst thing to ever happen to you."

His lips brushed over my cheek as he started to pull away.

In a moment of sheer, bold will—or panic—I grabbed him before he could take a step. His gaze snapped down to where my fingers circled his wrist then slowly crept up to my face, leaving a ripple of goose bumps over my skin.

"I'd risk it," I said.

There was a full shift in his mood. The moment my fingers made contact with him, he'd gone from playfully amused to bewildered. But now, there was something new there. A challenge. Or maybe curiosity. Either way, the heat from his gaze hollowed out my stomach.

He didn't speak, just took the tray from my hand and set it on the chair he'd been sitting on. Then, he led me to the back of the club. It was darker and less crowded, but the moment I started to worry about being seen making out with a celebrity, he pressed his palm to the wall and pushed. As if magically, a perfect rectangular cutout in the wall popped open. We slipped inside, the crease in the wall just large enough for us to pass through, before he pulled it closed behind him.

The secret room was small, just big enough for a

love seat and two large sitting pillows on the floor. A dim wall sconce was the only source of light, but I was betting that anyone who knew this room existed didn't care that you could hardly see your hand in front of your face.

"This is cozy," I said, my awkward words thudding against the soundproofed floor.

"Don't lose your nerve now that you've got what you'd been wishing for." His dark voice fully engulfed me.

My spine straightened. He was right. The buzz of my confidence had faltered for a moment, but I had him all to myself. I was going to seize the moment because I had fantasized about Ezra fucking St. Croix since I was a teenager.

I reached up and cupped the back of his neck to bring his mouth to mine. His soft lips tasted like whiskey, nicotine, and power. When my tongue slipped between them, he welcomed me with broad, slow swipes that stirred a tension in my core and instantly soaked my panties. He tangled his fingers through my hair, and the palms of his hands cradled my jaw and brought our kiss deeper. The overwhelming flood of endorphins made my head swim.

He held the back of my neck with one hand as the other smoothed down my back to my ass. With a firm grip, he hoisted me up to wrap my legs around his waist and pinned me to the wall. My already short dress hiked up to my hips and bared my ass for him. The front of his jeans stretched tight over his hard cock and pressed against the very thin fabric of my panties.

He gave me another rough grind of his hips, and I gasped, but the sound was quickly eaten up by his demanding mouth. He wasn't in a hurry, but every moment of his lips on mine built a furious, sinful feeling that had me drowning. I was desperate to feel him closer, deeper.

His mouth slipped down my jaw as two fingers pushed the soaked silk of my underwear to the side and brushed my eager center.

"Oh God," I moaned at the circles he made.

He grunted then pulled away. His craving eyes focused on my lips.

"This is your last warning," he said, his voice husky. "Because once I've had a taste of you, you're mine."

"I'm not afraid of you, Ezra." I was breathless, but it was answer enough for him.

He groaned and let me down to my feet. "On your knees."

I did as he demanded.

The cold floor sent a shiver through me and bit into my exposed knees. My hands smoothed up his thighs to the button of his jeans. I rolled my eyes up to his face and was met with an icy blue stare. He placed a hand on the wall behind me, his stance broad and expectant.

Our eyes locked in our next dare: a game of how far I was willing to go and how far he could push me till my breaking point. But I'd probably never get this chance again. It was now or never.

The button popped open easily, and the zipper didn't catch on its way down. His fingers curled around the bottom of his shirt and pulled it up to clutch it to his chest. I took in every tattoo and ripple of muscle I had only seen in magazines. His most well-known tattoo was at eye level with me now. The black rope-shaped cursive letters, bracketed by the notches at his hips, read, "Giddy Up."

I bit down on my lower lip, to keep a giggle of anxiety trapped in my throat, then pulled his jeans down and past the perfect outline of the impressive girth showing through his tight briefs.

My hands shook; there was no going back or losing my nerve. I needed my A game because it would have been shameful to give this man and that cock a bad blow job. He pulsed, the obvious jerk from his swollen head a silent plea for relief. I took one last steadying breath and pulled at the thick elastic band at his waist just when a pounding sound came from the other side of the door, making me shriek.

"Occupied!" Ezra boomed above my head. He looked over his shoulder at the source of the interruption but didn't move from his position over me.

The door opened, and a voice flooded in with the loud EDM music from outside. "My office. Now."

The door closed without another command, and Ezra's shoulders fell with a sigh. He pushed away from the wall he'd caged me against and offered me his hand. By the time I'd gotten to my feet and straightened my dress, he'd already zipped and buttoned his pants.

He reached for my hip, bringing me into him. That hand slinked up to my chest then came to rest on my neck. He ran his other hand through his hair, the wicked, rebellious strands falling perfectly over his temples. He dipped down and pressed the lightest kiss to my lips.

"What's your name, beautiful?"

"Pru," I squeaked, still breathless and slightly lightheaded from horny whiplash.

"Wait for me at the bar, Pru. We'll finish what we started." His tongue ran over my bottom lip.

I nodded, or at least I tried. His hand at my throat cupped my chin and gently forced my gaze to focus on his.

"That's my good girl."

As if those words weren't enough to make me melt into a puddle, the kiss he gave me before turning and walking away left me boiling from the inside out. I was no longer solid matter as I floated out to wait at the bar.

2

GAAP

If I had known Sitri was having a meltdown, I wouldn't have come to him for help. The Hunter who'd cornered me in Japan, of all places, had been following me for sixteen months. The trace he had put on me was stunted for the moment, but it would wear off soon.

I needed a prince for this kind of magic. But I owed Ipos a debt I wasn't ready to take on yet. Stolas was too preoccupied with his new plaything, and after the last run-in with Seere, it was more likely that Heaven and Hell would be reunited than him helping me.

No. It had to be Sitri.

He would just have to shake himself out of his tantrum and help me.

In his office, his Watcher lapdog stood behind his desk with a woman under his arm. She wasn't human, but she wasn't a demon either. She was a Reaper. Another grey being, like Watcher Angels, she wasn't welcome among the angels in Heaven but didn't truly belong in Hell. Her sole purpose was to usher mortals to their final destination. Whatever she was doing with Sitri and Ezequiel, it was a mess I didn't want to get involved with.

"It's been a long time, Gaap." Sitri sat with his fingers steepled, his chin resting on top. He watched me closely. "Or have you become too accustomed to Ezra St. Croix?"

He had a right to distrust me after what I'd done the last time I had breezed into Los Angeles, but I wasn't here to hash out my past mistakes with my brothers. I was running from a more pressing problem. "Scoff all you want, but I haven't had to hear my true name in decades. You can appreciate how any name moaned just right can feel more powerful than your gifts, can't you, Prince of Lust?"

"What do you want, Gaap?" Ezequiel chimed in harshly.

Cutting him a warning glance, I cleared my throat and spoke to Sitri. "A Hunter has been tracking me. I need your help, brother."

"Brother?" Ezequiel interjected once again. "You abandon your duties, leave every one of us behind to clean up your mess, and now that you need him, he is your brother?"

"Do you really want to start comparing abdications of duty, Watcher?" I snapped back.

"Enough." Sitri got to his feet, becoming a wall between Ezequiel and me. "Gaap, where is the Hunter?"

"Here. In Los Angeles." I was unable to look either Sitri or Ezequiel in the eye.

Sitri's head sank as he let out a curse. He pounded his fist on the desk, breaking a glass of liquor, which cut into his flesh. Dark blood gushed, and the Reaper bolted to Sitri and to tend to his wound. She took off her black T-shirt and wrapped his hand tight. He didn't bat her away. Instead, he looked at her in surprise that she would come to his side so easily.

Their silent exchange held more complication than I had brought to Sitri's doorstep.

He lifted his uninjured hand to her cheek and brought her temple to his lips, a rare show of intimate affection from the prince of meaningless, impassioned sex.

"I'm fine," he said, bringing her eyes to meet his.

She tied off the blood-damp shirt and stepped back to Ezequiel, who was waiting with one of The Deacon's sweatshirts. He held it up and assisted it over her head and down her body before wrapping his arm around her once again.

"Sitri, I didn't know where else to go," I explained.

"Have you completely lost grip on reality? You lured the Hunter here to Los Angeles?" Ezequiel's anger was present, but his volume had dimmed—probably for the sake of the Reaper currently watching her prince from her Watcher's arms.

"I knew the club would be the safest place to be for now." I bounced between him and Sitri.

"Just kill him," the Reaper said.

The three of us gawked at her. Sitri dropped his head with a forceful sigh at her ignorance.

"If it were that simple, I would have when he cornered me in Yokohama," I answered.

"Killing him would be seen as an act of war. Every Hunter and lesser angel would be up our asses," Ezequiel explained and pulled her into his side. "No, it's best to influence or spell him away. Not raise any flags or cause any closer inspection."

I'd never expected Ezequiel and Sitri to share a lover for longer than a night. I was more surprised that she was a Reaper. I looked her over. She was attractive, but other than that, I didn't see the appeal. Neutral beings could not be corrupted or bent to my will. Sitri and Ezequiel were bound to be wrapped around her scythe until she was forced to take her position in the grand design.

"He has warded his skin. Not just ink, but

scarred with hellfire." I'd seen the marks myself and had felt their repellent power when I'd tried to fend him off in the catacombs of Rome months before our last encounter.

The Reaper scoffed. "That's a little overkill."

Ezequiel gave her a sideways glance.

"What do you expect us to do about it?" Sitri cuts back to me. "Hide you until he grows too old to pace the threshold of The Deacon?"

I raked my fingers through my hair then roughed the back of my neck, clasping my hands together to rest there. The pulling sensation at my nerves did little to calm the knots growing tighter in my chest.

He'd caught and kept on my trail for the span of continents. The agreements between Heaven and Hell would not keep him from breaching the doors of the club.

Sitri tossed me a set of keys; the tag on the metal ring read 406. "You'll stay in one of the spare apartments upstairs and we'll spread word that you've gone back to Hell. He won't retreat immediately, so make yourself at home until he gives up."

"I'll call Eligos. Perhaps he can help," Ezequiel announced. It was an oddly kind idea.

Eligos, a duke of Hell, would be a useful being to have in my corner. He could conceal me and the magic signature the Hunter was following, but it would be useless if the persistent Hunter was as stub-born as he appeared.

"You have my eternal gratitude, brother," I said to Sitri.

"Don't make me regret this," Sitri said as he rounded his desk and walked me to the door. "You may have made a name for yourself as a rock god among the humans, but our brothers believe you to be a coward and not worthy of your title."

"Prince of Sloth returning to his throne by force. Who would have thought that day would come?" Ezequiel's smug words had me biting my tongue.

Ezequiel needed to be put in his place, but at the moment, I needed Sitri on my side more than I needed to see Ezequiel's face bloodied. I unclenched my jaw and rolled my neck. The tense muscles in my shoulders ached, but what better way to destress than to fuck my new friend, Pru, until the sun came up? If I had to hide out for days, I might as well find a way to pass the time.

After leaving Sitri's office, I scanned the crowd around the bar for Pru. The swarm of bodies ordering and waiting for drinks wouldn't thin for another few hours, but I wanted to get out of here as quickly as I could.

I'd almost given up when I saw a flash of green eyes look at me from around the arm of a large human man towering over her. The guy swayed drunkenly, his face red and eyes glassy. She attempted to step away but was held tighter. Most human men disgusted me, and this one chose the wrong woman to impose himself on.

Her eyes widened, possibly from the angry fire in my eyes. But it wasn't she who would feel the ache of a broken jaw in the morning. His fingers spread and squeezed her ass cheek, the fabric of her dress bulging in his grip.

My feet were moving before I heard her yelp, but as I reached them, the crack of her hand across his face brought a wicked grin to mine. The man crumpled to the floor.

She was feisty in more ways than I'd expected.

"There you are, beautiful," I said over the wails of the man who'd been taken down by a dainty woman.

He got to his knees in time to see me wrap my arms around her shoulders from behind. Pru and I watched him stagger to his feet. I could feel her shaking with fury against my chest, but he would not see her fall apart. He would only be permitted to see the blurred image of her holding her head up high with an internationally known rock star draped over her and staring down at him like he was nothing but a roach.

I pulled her hair back from the shell of her ear,

kissed her neck, then said loud enough for him to hear, "Is there a problem here?"

"No—she's a total slut, man. She came on to me," the soon-to-be-dead man slurred as he cupped his cheek.

"Is that true, Pru?" I cooed, dropping a kiss on her jaw. "Last I checked, you were only a slut for me."

I slid a hand down her stomach and pulled her closer, the tips of my fingers grazing the sensitive flesh above her cunt. She sucked in a breath but held her head high.

"N-no, Ezra," she answered, her voice not quite loud enough.

I used two fingers to pull at her dress and leaned into her ear. "Louder. Or I'll have to show him what he'll be missing tonight."

"I'm your little slut, baby."

A guttural groan rose up from my chest, and blood rushed to my cock.

"I need to get you alone. Now." I tucked her into the nook under my arm and led her away from the crowd that had been drawn to the scene.

Pru didn't question where we were going when I stopped in front of the elevator hidden in the corner of the club. Once inside, I pressed the floor button that matched the number on the set of keys, then I turned to see Pru watching me.

"Did he hurt you?" I leaned against the handrail and raked my hand through my hair to busy my fingers.

I would be inside of her soon enough. After being groped, she probably needed a moment to calm down and realize she was safe.

Well, safer than she would've been with the drunk asshole human.

"No. He was a dick, but he didn't hurt me." She pushed off the wall and stepped in front of me. "Thanks for not standing me up."

Her hands smoothed up my chest to clasp around my neck. The heels of her shoes brought her just below my chin, but that didn't stop her from pulling my face down to hers. Her perfume mingled with her cooled sweat from dancing and the other bodies that had ground against her earlier.

"I told you, once I tasted you, you were mine," I reminded her, but she wouldn't know the implications of that promise until I finally got her clothes off.

Her eyes searched mine, and she appeared mesmerized and anxious all at once. It was a look I'd seen hundreds of times, but on Pru, it sent a skitter of excitement through me. It had been years since I was approached by a singular fan in a place the paparazzi wouldn't hear about in the morning.

Maybe it was her willingness to please me. Or it

could have been the circumstances of my imprisonment inside of The Deacon for the foreseeable future. Either way, when our lips met and her tongue stroked over mine, I knew I needed her for longer than the remainder of the night.

The low chime of the elevator announced our arrival, and the doors opened to my floor. I led her down the short hallway and opened the apartment, allowing her to enter first. My hand flattened against the wall and searched for the light, but she tugged me away by the fingers.

We'd let the city lights streaming in from the huge wall of windows be enough.

The dark silhouette of her hips and ass in the bedroom doorway had my mouth watering. I heard the soft rustling of fabric being swept away, followed by the drop of her shoes.

I pulled my shirt over my head, threw it over my shoulder, and followed her to the bed. Finally catching her waist in my hands, I pulled her to me. She was soft, warm, and the smell of endorphins was seeping through her pores.

She yanked on the waistband of my jeans. "Take these off."

"Not yet."

I wanted her to beg, but first, I wanted to hear her pant my name. Her hand cupped my hardening cock through the tight pants and she whimpered for me.

Our mouths met in the dark and devoured each other.

"It's about to get rough, beautiful," I gruffed into her lips. "Do you want a safeword?"

She didn't answer, just kissed my jaw then down my neck and chest.

"Pru." The sternness of my tone gave her pause. "Safeword."

"Okay. What's the safeword?" she answered, out of breath.

"Apple."

3
PRU

pple? What sort of hippie shit was apple?

"Fine. Now will you take your pants off and fuck me?" I couldn't wait any longer.

The moment he'd saved me from that jerk at the bar, I'd been ready to suck him off in the middle of the club.

The guy who had felt me up had offered to buy me a drink while I waited for Ezra. I'd stopped drinking years ago, so when I turned the guy down, he asked if I wanted to dance. With another declined offer, he immediately started grabbing my ass and cornering me so I couldn't leave.

Now that I had Ezra alone in a dark room, I was ready to show him my appreciation and devotion as an adoring fan for over a decade.

He had me standing at the end of the bed. His

fingers caged my hips, and the smell of his skin had my panties soaked already.

"So eager for me." He groaned into the crown of my head. "Sit."

I did as he commanded and waited for him to make another.

The room was dark, but the lights from the skyscrapers, streetlights, and never-ending lines of traffic were enough to see his impossibly bright blue eyes intent on my face. I leaned forward, and he watched as my tongue circled the soft spot along his hip bone and my fingers pulled the button of his pants open.

He did me the favor of removing everything but his boxer briefs. The soft material hugged the tops of his thighs.

The sight made me salivate and my pussy ache.

I rolled my gaze up to his, pleading for permission to pull his shorts down. He groaned, and I took that as encouragement. His swollen head peeked over his waistband, then the rest of him stood at full attention with a subtle bounce. He was glorious. The prettiest cock I'd ever seen.

Every rumor I'd heard about Ezra having a piercing between his legs was right, but I'd had no idea he had more along the underside of his shaft. I couldn't tell exactly how many yet, but I wanted to count them with my tongue.

He cupped the back of my head with one hand and fisted the base of himself with the other to guide the throbbing tip into my mouth. Salty, slick fluid coated my taste buds, and I hummed as the first, second, third, then fourth set of metal balls slid over my tongue. They massaged back and forth as I bobbed and sucked. I didn't want to hurt him, but he had given me a safeword.

When I started moving my head with more vigor, sucking at the tip with each stroke, he moaned my name, which only built up the ego I already had. I knew I was good at this. I was proud of how quickly I could get a man off with my mouth. The technique had been honed by many men: not too much saliva, some light suction with the addition of friction closer to the tip. That was my surefire way of getting any man to come in a matter of minutes.

I didn't want to chance Ezra getting off and not being able to fuck him properly. There was no way he was going to want me to stay the night, so the odds of a second round were slim if he was like most other men I'd been with.

"Oh fuck, Pru." His lust-thick words stirred butterflies in my stomach.

I gave his head one last suck then licked each rung of his ladder slowly, playing with the seven bars with the tip of my tongue. His fingers weaved through my hair and pulled me away gently. When he dipped his face close to mine, our shared breath lit a fire in my chest. I couldn't place the emotion in his captivating eyes, but something inside of me was telling me to run. Fast.

"You're so good at that." His throaty voice vibrated over my lips and all the way down to the throbbing between my legs.

The urge of self preservation in my chest didn't ease completely, but his next two words made me forget every twinge of doubt I had. "Lie back."

I did.

My dress, shoes, and reservations were lying on the floor somewhere between the bed and the front door. After settling into the plush duvet, I was on full display to him.

He stood at the edge of the bed, staring down at me and stroking himself slowly. My heart skipped a beat just from looking at him.

Ezra wasn't just rock-star hot.

He was sex-god hot.

His dark, slick hair was tousled to the side from his fingers. Tattoos ran from his neck all the way down to his toes, each one beautiful, intricate, and crisp against the patches of skin peeking between them.

He was gorgeous, but it was more than that. He was magnetic. His voice, his attitude, the way he carried himself. He didn't just play the role of a musician; he stood for a cause. His art had always been about standing up for the masses and turning his critique of our corrupt society into poetry he sang to stadiums. To thousands of screaming admirers.

But for tonight, he was all mine.

"You're so beautiful." The dark inflection of his voice skittered through my insides.

"I'm cold." I was lying but the goose bumps over my skin wouldn't give me away.

He gave me a wicked smile and crawled toward my body. His lips grazed the tender skin on my thighs, my stomach, my chest. A wanton noise broke over my tongue and earned me another heart-melting smile.

"Oh, baby." He paused for a soft and slow kiss. "I am going to ruin you."

Please do.

I'd never wanted something so desperately in my life. My hips shifted under him, begging for friction.

"Ezra," I pleaded, another swarm of butterflies whirling inside my whole being.

His fingers framed my jaw, lifting my eyes to meet his. "Shh, just a little bit more."

Torture. This man was torturing me.

His fingers trailed down my neck, through the valley of my breasts, and over the sensitive spots of my stomach to the needy heat between my legs.

27

"You're so wet for me." He spoke into my lips, making my breath hitch and my hips squirm.

He played slow circles over my throbbing clit and coaxed a moan. The higher the tension he built, the less patient I became. I wanted him to fill me up, to feel each piercing against my spasming walls.

His lips and tongue tempted my mouth as he worked his fingers in a masterful rhythm. I groaned in desperation, and my hips searched for the heel of his hand to chase the building orgasm. His deep, gruff laugh vibrated along my tongue, followed by the lightening of pressure from his hand.

The slow build had every nerve throbbing, but the sudden change was almost painful. His teeth nipped at my shaking bottom lip, not hard but not distracting enough.

Finally, his fingers whirled larger circles around their previous track.

I was soaked, needy, and frustrated. He was toying with me, edging me close to the peak then backing off if I so much as groaned or bucked my hips.

I reached between us when the build became too much, only for him to snatch my wrist and put it over my head. His thigh gave me the leverage to grind against.

"Do you want to be mine, Pru?"

The pounding of my blood against my eardrum almost drowned out his husky whisper.

"Yes," I panted, so close to the orgasm that had been so hard to catch.

"That doesn't sound convincing. I think you can be more persuasive."

In a quick shift, he slid down and threw my knees over his shoulders. Hot breath brushed over my swollen flesh he had ruthlessly brought to life.

"If my fingers got you this wet," he said, watching me from over the top of my belly, "I wonder what my tongue could do."

His lips parted, and his tongue flattened over my clit in one long, broad stroke. A satisfied purr came from deep in his chest. "Fucking delicious."

He flicked, sucked, then paused when I wiggled closer. I had hoped he would have mercy on me when he changed our position, but he was more in control this way, and he was loving every bit of it.

Another stroke, then he sucked. I bit down on my lip to hold in any sound that would make him continue this wicked game. It would be worth the agony. He wouldn't be so cruel as to leave me wanting, would he?

No. I was close. Closer and higher than he'd allowed before. His lips hardened around my clit and rolled it around, over and over, until I was cursing and shaking.

"Just a little bit more, baby. Can you hold on for me?" Two fingers slipped inside, and his thumb pressed hard against my clit.

I grunted. "Ezra. Please."

"You want me to stop, Pru?" His thumb released and was replaced by his mouth once again.

He pumped his fingers in and out of my pussy slowly.

Too slowly.

"Oh God. I can't." My voice echoed through the room, and he sucked harder before stopping.

"You want to be mine, don't you?"

"Yes. Fuck yes, Ezra."

I looked down to see a broad and menacing smile over his glazed lips. "Tell me, then, beautiful. Tell me you're mine."

He lowered his mouth, and his fingers picked up the pace. Each pounding thrust from his wrist was chorused with a pull or suck from his lips, and my body hurtled toward the tipping point. The higher I rose, the more fearful I became of the fall. I'd never been so wound up, and every tingling inch of my skin was buzzing with the expectation of climax.

He pressed an arm over my hips to hold me in place. His mouth worked faster until the pressure became unbearable and I was crashing around his fingers and clawing at the sheets for relief.

"That's my girl. Give me one more. Give me

everything," he said, my stomach flipping at the words.

"I can't," I choked out through a moan.

But I was already building for another hard and fast plunge. My eyes rolled, and a gush of warm liquid spilled as I came apart on his face again.

Dazed and spent, I propped myself up on my elbows and looked down at the mess Ezra had brought out of me. The sheets were soaked, but he didn't move or look bothered. In fact, he looked proud.

Of himself. Of me. Maybe both.

My blood was coursing through my veins, but the adrenaline was ebbing, leaving my limbs weak. He looked down at his fingers that had stilled inside of me then back up to me with an almost playful look. He dipped his chin and sucked at my aching, wet center.

"I didn't hear you beg to be mine, Pru." His voice was dark and cocky.

He pulled me closer by my hips, taking the strength from my arms, and put me flat on my back once again. His fingers pumped deep before I found the air to moan. I came with no hesitation, and the crash had no time to subside before he was bringing me to the cusp again. My thighs squeezed and convulsed around his head at another orgasm. I cried out his name, but it only egged him on.

"Please, I want to be yours. Please," I managed through yet another climax.

"That's my girl." He purred, licking softly over my clit.

He got to his knees between my legs and stroked himself. My mouth watered at the sight of him over me, his cock hard for me.

"I'm going to fuck this pretty pussy until you can't walk straight. Do you remember what to say if you can't take it?"

If he hadn't just said he was going to fuck me until I couldn't handle it anymore, I would have swooned.

He leaned down, lining up his cock with my entrance, and kissed me slowly.

"I remember," I breathed, gripping the sheets and determined to take everything he wanted to give me and more.

He edged in. The short popping sensation of each piercing hitched my breath.

"Oh fuck. You're so big." My voice sounded more like a squeak than actual words.

"Eyes on me, beautiful." His heavy breath hit my ear, and I did as he demanded. "Take a deep breath and don't you dare look away."

His eyes intensified, and he took an audible inhale that made his shoulders rise. I took in a lungful of him, and we breathed through the slow sinking of his cock inside of me. My walls pulsed around him, and I was already so close to coming.

"That's it," he whispered over my lips and released a slow exhale. "This pussy was made for me and I'm going to earn it."

"God, yes," I groaned as his hips circled.

The first thrust was slow and heavy. He eased me into harder and faster poundings until the whole bed was quaking and I was close to having an out-of-body experience.

Who was screaming his name so loud? She sounded like she'd gone mad.

His mouth over mine tamped down the banshee who was obviously possessing me. I bit into the side of my cheek, partly to keep myself from bringing the ceiling down on us but also to keep me conscious. It was all too much.

"Ezra. God, Ezra. Fuck."

This chant was the only coherent English I was able to speak. I was coming undone again, and it was becoming increasingly painful with each new wave of pleasure.

"You're mine." Another punishing crash of his hips. "Tell me."

"I'm yours, Ezra. I'm yours."

"*I'm yours, Gaap,*" he demanded. "Say it."

"I'm yours!"

"Say my true name." Every syllable came with another thrust. "Gaap."

"I'm yours, Gaap."

He broke through some sort of tether and unleashed himself fully. It was hard to believe he had been holding back. With one swift motion, I was on my stomach and being hauled to the side of the bed. My legs dangled off the mattress as he took me from behind, the balls of his piercings hitting new targets of pleasure I never knew were there.

I unraveled into nothing.

His fingers gripped and held me in place as he used me. And I loved every second of it. My muscles shook with jolts of electricity and the ache of being drained of all their strength. It was over an hour before I finally gave him what I knew he really wanted.

"Apple." I wept from delirious overstimulation. "Please. Apple."

His body stopped immediately. The sweat of his chest was cold on my back as he pulled me up against him.

Ezra kissed my drenched temple and helped me into the bed. Time was whirling either too fast or too slow because what felt like a second later, he was handing me a bottle of cold water. I chugged it down and let it cool my body inside and out with small streams escaping my lips and running over my chest and down my stomach.

"Are you okay?" He grinned down at me from where he stood next to the bed.

I sneered up at him. "Why does it sound more like you're gloating than actually checking on my well-being?"

I reached for his half full bottle of water and he handed it to me without hesitation, "You're breathing. Not bleeding. I'd say you've fared better than most."

I let that skip right by and drained the rest of his water. His smug expression only grew more insufferable. I tossed the empty bottles at him, and he easily batted them away.

"Are you going to lie down, or are you waiting for me to leave?" I tried to hide the preemptive disappointment in my voice at the last thought.

The hunger in his eyes could have eaten me whole. "If you're even thinking about leaving, then my job isn't done."

"I'm going to need a nap before round two," I said.

He crawled over to me on hands and knees and planted a soft but possessive kiss on my lips.

"I'll give you everything you'll ever need and more, Pru."

And I believed him.

4

GAAP

Pru had sealed her fate when she'd screamed my name as I'd fucked her raw.

Declaring she was mine and calling out my true name were all I needed to take ownership of her and her soul.

She was mine and would be a distraction and a tool at my disposal. Alessio wouldn't dare harm a human woman to get to me. It would go against everything he stood for and mark his soul with a bloodred stain. Every demon in Hell who came across his path would be waiting for their pound of flesh.

Speaking of pounding, there was an awful sound coming from the front door.

It couldn't have been Sitri; he had keys to every unit in the building. My next guess was Eligos, though he wasn't typically so intrusive.

I unfurled myself from Pru's arms and pulled on my boxers so I could answer the discourteous lout with decency. The sheet draped over Pru's ass dipped low, and the slightest view of her cunt peeked out between her thighs. She was exhausted and would be sore when she woke up. But that wouldn't stop me from fucking her at least once more before feeding her breakfast.

The infernal knocking grew louder until I made my way to open the door.

"For fuck's sake, Eli, you sure have become impatient since I saw you last—"

"Not this time," Ipos said. His booming presence silenced me before his words. "I see you haven't changed a bit. Slacking off while everyone else cleans up your mess." He took a step inside and looked down the hall at the line of clothing leading to the bedroom.

"And you are still tall and intimidating. Neither of us made room for growth, it would seem," I said, bored already. "If you're here to demand I take back my legions and territory, I'm a bit preoccupied at the moment. With being hunted by a saintly priest and all."

I hadn't looked around the apartment last night, but it was fairly small with an open floor plan. The living room was the bulk of the space, and there was a kitchen off to the side. Faux brick lined the long wall that connected the kitchen and living space.

In the light of day, the apartment could have used a good cleaning.

I walked over to a cabinet for a glass and filled it with water, watching Ipos as I chugged it without a breath.

"I came to ask the Watcher a question, but Sitri was eager to let me know that you were here. Sounded like he wanted to get rid of you as soon as he could."

"Can't blame him. I've not been the smartest of us." I shrugged. "And I do tend to leave a mess of the dwellings he loans me."

Ipos smirked. The lines of his thoroughly sunned face were defined, like well worn leather. The desert he'd been hiding away in hadn't only rotted his brain, but he looked older—and worn.

"That's what you'd like us all to think, isn't it? That the Prince of Sloth was too dim-witted to see the effects he inflicted on those around him. We both know you're much cleverer than our brothers suspect."

Unlike Sitri, Stolas, or even Orobas, Ipos saw more than visions of the future. He could see through the thin veil of incompetence I'd shrouded myself in all these years. Being the Prince of Sloth gave me the perfect excuse to not live up to my fullest potential. My brothers had the natural talent to rule over their territories and the eagerness to succeed in their own missions. But it blinded them to my intentions. It was easy for them to write me off as a waste of a title, and their taking up of my responsibilities—of my legions—in my absence only furthered their personal agendas.

Sitri had taken on several of my legions and put them to work on the streets of L.A. to attract the most beautiful and most powerful humans to The Deacon.

Stolas and Orobas used their allotted legions to build their empire.

But Ipos had put my remaining legions to work overseeing my other obligations: harvesting souls in all corners of North America and keeping his location as cloaked as possible.

He may have not abandoned his duties in the same way that I had, but we were both guilty of misusing our titles. Considering, however that I might need every prince's help, including his, it was the wrong time to bring up those facts.

I perked a brow in his direction. "What brings you out of the desert, Prince of Pride?"

"Lucifer has sent me to find something that was stolen from him." He sighed, obviously annoyed with his new mission. "You wouldn't happen to know anything about an ancient copper ring, would you?"

I cocked my head. That and the expression on my face were enough of an answer, but the questions buzzing between my ears made their way to my mouth. "Who in their right mind would steal an artifact from the all-powerful Emperor of Hell? And what would make this ring so valuable that he would send the all-knowing seer to look for it?"

"Your guess is as good as mine, but I have a feeling the magic surrounding the ring is hiding it very well. I can't manifest a full vision of its whereabouts, but I know that there is a magical signature emitting from it. It's faint here in Los Angeles, but it's close."

"How close?" I asked, invested in the mystery.

"It's in California. It hasn't crossed the desert to the east or the waters to the west," he said with a glint of silver around his irises, the *sight* bringing him a glimpse of the treasure he was seeking.

"What would someone use this ring for?"

If we knew the intent, perhaps the user would be easier to narrow down. If it were another demon, as foolish as that would be, they could be using it to pull off a great deal of damage to humanity, padding their soul count with a tragedy or natural disaster.

"Ezequiel didn't know exactly, but if it was once in the possession of a guardian angel, it could be used for good. Or some semblance of it."

"Lucifer was holding on to a weapon of . . .

good?" My interest was growing with each new detail.

"Whatever it was being used for, it is greatly missed." Ipos shook out his rusty, sun-tinted hair then tied it up on top of his head.

I narrowed an eye at him. He would fit right in on Venice Beach with the surfers and beach bums. But he was far too obsessed with titles and duty to be able to earn his spot among either group. Being called upon by Lucifer for this errand showed he wasn't off the grid as much as I had thought. That meant I could get away with not accepting my place in our ranks for a little while longer if I paid a few favors.

"Speak what you want from me and be on your way." I peered into the large bedroom and saw Pru had left the bed. "I have my own interests to attend to."

Ipos rolled his gold eyes and sighed heavily. "I need you to take a little trip down south. I'm going to go north. I have a small hunch that the Leviathan might know where the ring would be."

The Leviathan was an ancient beast that had once roamed the oceans with its mate. But when Father was wrathful and vain, he struck down the second beast and plagued the Leviathan to wander alone. The Leviathan was able to take possession of human bodies, and though he was never able to become whole himself, he hopped from vessel to vessel when needed.

"Where is he?" I asked.

"San Diego. La Jolla, to be more specific."

"Eligos will be here tonight. I can't leave until he cloaks me."

It wouldn't take long for Eli's spell to take hold, but there was a chance that Alessio would be able to see through the incantation and trail me down to San Diego.

Ipos rolled his eyes, unappeased by my delayed departure. "Fine. I'll text you the address."

E zra's voice had woken me up. Whoever had come to the door seemed angry, and I figured the best place for me to hide was in the shower. My hair was greasy, and my muscles hurt from dancing and fucking until dawn. Hot water ran over the new bruises on my lower back, hips, and thighs. Each one gave a satisfying sting when I touched it.

I'd always liked it rough, but being tossed around a bedroom was nothing compared to the night I'd spent with Ezra. He'd given me at least a dozen orgasms, and most by force. The memory sent my blood pounding through my veins and to the tortured clit between my legs.

How could I possibly want to be touched after all that? Maybe I was greedier than I thought.

I swept two fingers up my inner thigh and over

another set of bruises just below where my legs met. He'd made those while he'd taken me from behind, holding all my spent weight in his hands as he pounded into me. I wished I could have watched him use me until he was slick with sweat and thoroughly sated.

"I hope you're thinking of me." The devil himself stepped into the shower with a smile that could bring me to my knees.

"Maybe," I answered "Or maybe not."

I let myself take in the full sight of his naked body, and I swore I started drooling.

Fuck. He was a wet dream come to life.

The playful curl of his lips turned into a lascivious line. In a simple relaxation of muscle, his expression shifted to a sinister sort of sexy. There was more than hunger in his gaze. This wasn't horny or even sexual. It was power. Ownership.

The thrill I got from that idea overpowered the red flags and warning alarms going off in my gut. Clarity of this new dynamic—and the rabble of butterflies in my stomach—stole all reason from my senses. And as long as he looked at me like that, I would play the doleful idiot who hung myself on his every movement.

"Now that you are mine, every orgasm you have belongs to me and will be provided only by me."

My throat tightened around unsure words and

strangled them down. I wasn't going to disagree with him, but I was starting to get concerned about my missing feminine rage.

"Spread your legs for me, beautiful," he said. "Now."

My thighs tensed. I was so sore, and the aching pulse his voice caused was already building tension in my stomach. I shook my head, and at my rebellion, he forced his knee between mine and pried me open. I whined and bit down on my lip as his fingers circled slowly over my clit and my back pressed against the cool shower tile. His sadistic smile was back, and all the fight I could strum up was proving to not be enough.

The water hit his chest and sprayed over my face, making me choke. I turned away to take a deep breath and clawed into his wrist as his pace quickened. He leaned into the stream to shield me, his hand firm above my head.

He dipped low next to my cheek. The echo of our bodies and the water intensified the sound of my needy moans and my whimper when his fingers slipped inside of me. I ground my hips into his palm.

"That's right, Pru." His voice pinged off the tile. "Beg for me."

With every pump, the build of my climax teetered me in and out of focus. I was on the edge and at his mercy. He laughed deep in his chest. He'd already mastered how to bring my body so close to the breaking point then snap me back from the edge and plunge me into pent-up frustration. The game was becoming predictable, but I fell for it each and every time.

"I know." He pulled his hand away, leaving me feeling empty and desperate. "You can't help yourself, can you? Such a needy little slut for me."

"Fuck you," I said through my teeth.

He watched me closely with his bottom lip between his teeth. His hand slipped down the wall and circled around my neck, his fingers tightened against my pressure points.

"I should fuck that sass out of your mouth." His voice was dark and daring, but pleased.

I swallowed and my throat rippled under his palm. My blood pumped hard, and a small panic started to build where pleasure was only moments ago.

"Ezra . . ."

He didn't answer.

Firm grip in place, he pulled me away from the shower wall and turned me around so that his hard cock pressed into my lower back. His hand around my throat now tilted my chin up, forcing our eyes to meet over my shoulder.

With his free hand, his fingers trailed down my stomach and roughed over my clit in demanding strokes. I gripped his forearm, feeling the rhythm in his muscles. The hot water pounded against my sternum and over my tight nipples. His wet hair fell in a black curtain around his eyes and dripped cool droplets onto the top of my shoulder. The temperature contrast added to the onslaught of stimulation.

"I own every orgasm, Pru," he repeated, but this time his words held a new, possessive meaning. "And I'm going to take what's mine."

The high I was getting from his dominance and the way he relentlessly circled my clit convinced me that I did owe him my pleasure. Why wouldn't I want to give into his every whim when the reward was well worth my free will.

"Maybe I need to tattoo my name on this tight pussy so you remember who it belongs to."

"Isn't that bad luck or something?" I sassed back.

"I'm the worst thing that could have happened to you, beautiful. And luck had nothing to do with it."

His hips pulled back and the thick head of his cock rubbed over my center. I was swollen but aching for more. I wriggled my hips, both trying to coax him inside and push him away. I couldn't make up my mind about whether I wanted to give in to him or if I wanted to protest.

He didn't give me another moment to decide. He pushed slowly with a hissing curse. "Oh fuck."

He shuddered behind me, and my muscles tightened as another piercing made its way inside. I sucked in a breath with every rung until I was light-headed and clinging to his arms for dear life.

The throaty groans from his chest vibrated through me, and I answered with a mewl of my own. He'd worked himself down to his base and rocked his hips at first, then he shifted into full thrusts.

I cried out his name as I reached my orgasm, but he didn't slow to let me ride it out.

Instead, he let go of my throat and gripped my shoulder, pushing forward until my hands reached for the wall in front of me for support. He pounded furiously, one hand clamped to my hip and the other strumming my overstimulated clit until I was coming undone again.

"You come so easily for me." He grunted. "Again. Give me another."

My body writhed and crashed again at his whim. His fingers only stilled for the orgasm to recede before he beckoned another. The crushing waves of pleasure blinded me to any other concern except staying on my feet for him to finish with a thun-derous roar.

His hips bucked, rattled, then stilled as he filled me with his come until it dripped down my thighs to the drain below.

He pulled me up into his arms, and I rested my head on his chest to catch my breath and gain the strength to clean myself. We stayed silent under the water. Every nerve in my body vibrated with the aftereffects of that life-changing fucking.

How could anyone else push me to my limits like he had, break down those boundaries, then make me cry for more?

I was fucked.

6

GAAP

A lessio was not subtle about his stakeout. From the apartment window, I watched him pace for over an hour while Pru took a nap. I'd exhausted her, but it kept her from leaving. It would only be a few more hours until Eli agreed to meet me downstairs in The Deacon.

When Pru did wake, I had dinner waiting for her. She'd told me that she enjoyed Italian food, and I'd spent over a year in Sicily before Alessio had figured out a way to track down demons.

After sending one of the lesser demons from the club out to fetch ingredients, I tossed together the pasta and pomodoro sauce. Pru was dressed in one of my old T-shirts—which barely covered her ass— as I was setting our plates on the small dining table.

"Wow. This looks incredible." She looked over the plates and glasses of wine I'd poured. She picked hers up and put it on the counter. "I'm sorry, but I don't drink."

My eyes shot to her, and my hands stopped arranging marinated artichokes and olives on a platter.

"You weren't drinking last night?"

"No, I stopped drinking a few years ago. Drugs too." She frowned, but not out of sadness. She looked as though she had disappointed me. "To be honest, I probably wouldn't be here if I hadn't stopped when I did."

It wasn't that she abstained from alcohol that surprised me. It was that she'd had the courage to approach me without it. That type of confidence often came from a few shots of liquid courage.

I reached over to the wine she had discarded and dumped the contents into the sink. Her wide eyes followed me around the kitchen island to the glass remaining on the table, then as I went back to the sink to empty it as well.

"Sit," I said, lifting my chin toward the table. "Eat."

She bit down on her bottom lip to repress a smile and she did as she was told. Before I set down the last plate, she was twisting her fork into the nest of pasta and taking a bite. She hummed with pleasure and closed her eyes as she chewed.

"I can't believe you made this for me."

I handed her a bottle of water from the fridge then joined her. "I made you breakfast," I reminded her and took a mouthful of my own.

"Eggs, toast, and juice. That isn't perfectly al dente pasta and homemade sauce."

"For all you know, it's all a lie and I ordered out. You were asleep." I couldn't hold back the smile that the scrunch of her nose brought out of me.

"I woke up because you were loud. Pots and pans slammed around for thirty minutes before I got up."

She took another large bite, slurping a noodle, then licked the rich tomato sauce from her lips. I shot her an accusatory look and took a pull from my water bottle.

"You waited for half an hour before coming out?"

"I didn't want to get roped into helping." She shrugged. "And I was enjoying the free concert. You sing while you cook."

I chuckled and shook my head. "After last night, how could I not sing?"

My flattery turned her cheeks bright red, which brought back the image of her writhing in pleasure. Her body melting easily in my hands and giving into my every command. It had been too long since I'd taken a being to my bed, and longer still since I'd enjoyed bringing someone to the brink of madness.

"The shower today wasn't lyric worthy?" she teased.

"A whole record, beautiful." I gave her a wink, and I swore I saw her wiggle in a small show of hubris.

<hr />

Eli lounged in the VIP booth surrounded by beautiful humans. The duke of Hell didn't need the gifts of the princes to be a beacon for the lust- and alcohol-fueled patrons of The Deacon.

Sitri and his Reaper sat across from Eli, their arms wrapped around each other. The swoonful displays of affection occupied their attention and blocked out the busy club around them. Ezequiel was at the bar with Stolas and his newest human companion. It seemed that all of my brothers were dwelling in new bliss.

I watched Pru dancing with a group of strangers. I'd borrowed the dress she was wearing from Sitri's massive guest closet, deterring her from leaving and drawing any attention from the Hunter sulking outside.

Alessio had spelled me with a tracking beacon;

I'd found out the hard way that it meant that every soul I'd collected would be a breadcrumb to my whereabouts. I hadn't taken a soul since figuring it out. With Pru at my side, I could use her as a distraction or, if the situation escalated, a shield.

I needed Pru in my sight until Eli could procure a solution, however long that process would be.

If only I could get the duke to focus on me and not the woman currently dry humping him. The longer I sat waiting, the more anger brewed in my chest.

Music thrummed through the souls of everyone around us, entrancing them to move, touch, and feel as much as their bodies could handle. The low moans coming from the booth behind us proved how powerful Sitri had become in his new happiness. The magnitude of his influence flowed to every nook of The Deacon, and as such to my Pru.

The human man grinding against Pru's ass was rich, powerful in the human world, and handsome. Even with every luxury at his fingertips, I knew she had no interest in him over me, but the beast in my chest was not convinced enough to not demand that I rip off every one of his limbs. Each moment that she was touching someone else, the tighter the muscles in my fist and shoulders wound. He had his filthy hands on what was mine.

"I heard the Prince of Envy had resurfaced." Eli

chuckled, finally freed from the lap dance he'd been receiving. "He was missing for so long, I was starting to suspect he'd been truly vanquished. Any chance you've taken on some of his traits in his absence?"

I peeled my gaze away from Pru. "The sooner you cloak me from the Hunter, the safer The Deacon will be from my steadfast destruction." I tried—and failed miserably—to sound casual.

"You are not as bad as most." Eli gave a side-eyed glance to Sitri, who was obnoxiously slobbering all over his new plaything. "But I can help you. For a price."

He looked over at Pru, who had moved over to the one-man bar to grab an iced water. She'd chosen to be sober for her future and to save her reputation. It was an admirable trait to slay your own monsters and save yourself.

"I already own her soul," I glowered at Eli. "Choose someone else."

"You don't care for anyone else."

I cut him a lethal glance only to find him smug and imperious. He was masterful in the act of finding a being's weak spot and gouging it until it bled for him.

"I need her just in case your magic isn't strong enough." I took a pull from the second whiskey I'd ordered in the half hour of being down here.

He considered me. "My magic has never failed. Especially not against a human foe."

"Choose someone else," I repeated darkly.

Eli passed a curious glance between Pru and me again before amending his conditions. "Fine." He smirked at his own cunning. "The Hunter has a book in his arsenal that I want for my collection. It's bound by the hide of a hellhound and close to six hundred years old. You'll know it when you see it because it will know you."

I threw my hands out in exasperation. "The point of asking you for help was to avoid the Hunter, not confront or steal from him."

"No. The point is to shield your presence from him. To create a shroud around you so that you may roam freely—so you can become my pickpocket."

Eli, like others with similar abilities, spoke in riddles and half truths to those of us above his station. It was the only flex of his abilities he had and though annoying, it was expected. He didn't answer to any prince because he was much too valuable as a shared entity.

I had no choice but to take the deal. Even with Pru as a failsafe, I would only be buying myself time until Alessio cornered me again by whatever means he saw fit. It had been too close of a call to believe I would escape again.

"This better be a very powerful spell, Eligos."

"I'll deliver it to your apartment in an hour. I expect my payment by the end of the week."

With the agreement struck, Eli got to his feet to retrieve what he needed to conduct the protection spell. I took a long breath and let the hope settle in my chest.

Sitri lifted his head from the bubble of euphoria he'd been lost in. "This is where I leave you as well, brother. I have facilitated your agreement and survival. It's time for Ezequiel and me to take our Reaper upstairs to bed."

Sitri stood with the Reaper plastered to his side. Her dazzling brown eyes and thick lashes beamed up at her prince as if he'd breathed life into the sun. It was the type of affection I'd seen mimicked on tour for years, but it held more than blind admiration for his good looks and talents. It was intense, and when Ezequiel appeared and held out his hand to her, she paused to give him an equally bewitched look before she took his invitation gleefully and followed him to the elevator.

"Are you really satisfied? After all this time?" I watched Sitri's face brighten at the Reaper and Watcher waiting for him.

"More than you may ever know, brother," he said simply and walked away.

It wasn't for me to foresee whether his happiness would last the tests of time and love, but I believed him. Though he held power and influence over lust, there was a distinct difference between love and the temptations of the flesh. Whatever he, the Watcher, and the Reaper had between them had given my fellow prince an ease in his soul that I'd never seen in him. And for that, I was both grateful and disgusted.

The one weakness that had been deemed mine was dancing again, but she was watching me from where she swayed on the dance floor. A new man came up behind her, and she arched her back in response. With her eyes schooled on me, she reached an arm up and over her head and raked her fingers through his blond hair, bringing him even closer.

In return, he wrapped his arms around her waist and buried his face in the crook of her neck. Her jaw relaxed and her lips parted for his touch and my blood began to boil. I sat forward and made to stand when a lesser demon obstructed my view. She leaned down until her breasts teetered on the cusp of full exposure from the revealing dress she wore.

"Mind if I take a seat, my prince?" Her high-pitched voice rang over the music and her eyes fell to my lap.

I looked behind her to see Pru's eyes flare with heat. I crooked a smile and darkened my eyes at her. I gave the demon a slow nod and leaned back to give her a wide seat. With our eyes locked, Pru turned herself in her partner's arms so that her chest bumped against his torso. His hands traveled down her lower back to her ass, where he took a hard handful.

It wouldn't take but one more move for me to win this war Pru had started. She was either testing my patience or silently begging me for the domination she craved. Either way, she was toying with the possibility of me ripping that human's heart out of his chest with my bare hands and giving it to her as a gift. It may have been my move, but I gave her one more warning dip of my chin.

Against her better judgment, Pru pulled at the man's shoulder to bring his ear down to her and whispered something that made him blush. He looked at her as if she were going to start undressing right in front of him. She stole another glance at me, her nonverbal "checkmate."

The demon on my lap wiggled her ass over my groin, enticing my cock to wake for her—and failing. I brought my hand up to her cheek and fanned my fingers along the back of her head, then I brought her lips down a breath away from mine.

"Listen to me very carefully," I said loud enough for her to hear me. "I'm going to place my hand on your thigh and you're going to act as if I've just given you the greatest gift."

"You can do whatever you want to me, Prince Gaap," she cooed.

The sound of my true name on this creature's lips made my stomach clench in disdain.

"I would never lower myself to that, but you've found yourself in the middle of a battle of wills that I intend to win."

Hurt flashed over her face. Other demons likely would have accepted her offer, but I hadn't slept with another demon in centuries and never a lesser spirit.

I gave her a severe look, and she nodded eagerly. "Good."

My hand trailed up her thigh and under the hem of her dress but stopped short of the apex of her thighs. And like she was told, she dropped her head back and moaned. Her hips made generous circles over my crotch and she made a show of my will.

The rage in Pru's eyes quickly turned to something new. Mischief or spite. A hybrid of the two was a combination I hadn't expected. She pulled out of the arms that had been groping her and stormed off to the bar.

I stood, knocking the demon from my lap, and started across the short dance floor to stop her from destroying herself in an act of malice against me.

But she wasn't ordering a drink.

No. She had found a way to force me to show my hand.

On unsteady high-heeled shoes, Pru climbed from a stool up onto the glass of the bartop with loud encouragement from the patrons gathering around. Her hips dipped and circled to the beat of the music. Without much strain, anyone below her could see right up her dress to her bare pussy. I had convinced her to forgo underwear as a favor to me, but I was cursing myself now that she was putting herself on display for every horny bastard with a pulse.

I pushed my way through to the front of the mostly male crowd that didn't part easily for me. The slobbering morons were unaware of the ticking bomb they were scowling and hissing at.

"Pru, unless you want to be the reason that I turn this dance floor into a mosh pit of blood and broken bones," I called up to her. "I suggest you get down. Now."

"What's the matter, Ezra? Can't handle a crowd enjoying a show that isn't just for you?"

Several beings hooted and shouted their approval. She tugged at the skirt of her dress and brought it up her thigh a little more, and a man next to me held up his hand as if he were going to touch her. I reached out and took hold of his wrist then gave him a look of death. He quieted but didn't move away.

Pru bent at her waist to talk directly to me. "It's only a bit of fun, Ezra. They are just looking."

"I will rip their eyes from their sockets for looking

at what's mine," I said loud enough so everyone around us could hear.

She straightened and cocked her head down at me as if to say, "Prove it."

If Pru was going to test the limits, I would show her what lay beyond them.

I gripped the back of the disrespectful man's neck and with ease crashed his skull into the glass bartop. He yelped in pain before going limp. I released my hold and he slumped to the ground.

Screams erupted from the crowd. Onlookers scuttled about, trying to get him to his feet and away from the well-known lead singer who'd just rendered him immobile in half a second.

Pru didn't take her eyes off me. Not even to check if her admirer was conscious.

Our game was over with no true victor.

I reached up my hand and motioned with two fingers for her to take it. She stepped down onto a stool, and I gripped her thigh for stability—and to kiss its soft inner flesh. I looked up the line of her body to the prize I didn't earn with fervid need.

When I got her into the elevator, I dropped to my knees and hiked one of her legs over my shoulder to devour her. She panted and came quickly on my tongue before we'd made it up two floors. It was a race to pull one more from her before the door opened again. A challenge I won with only moments to spare.

"If you wanted my attention, you could have asked." I smiled up from between her thighs.

Her hips shifted, begging for more already. She would get more than she could handle soon enough.

I got to my feet and pinned her body to the wall, my hands circling her wrists to bring them above her head. My body was rigid against hers, and she groaned at the feeling of my cock. The sultry noise inspired visions of what pleasure I was going to inflict on her during another night she wouldn't forget.

She rolled her eyes up to mine with a mischievous grin. "It was more fun this way."

.

7
PRU

I didn't know how I was able to walk when I woke up the next morning. The only break Ezra took was to answer the door about an hour after we got back from the very passionate display down in the club.

When I'd started the game, I never expected him to injure someone just for looking at me, but I'd goaded him until the very end and was rewarded with the hottest night of my life.

Ezra cooked me breakfast then went down to the club to retrieve my purse from the locker system at the entrance. Not having any of my things for the last day and a half hadn't been difficult. It was almost like I'd taken a vacation from my life to go on some sort of tantric sex excursion. But I did have a life to get back to sooner or later.

When he gave my phone back, I had several

texts, voicemail messages, and way too many emails. The friends I'd come to The Deacon with only got worried last night when they hadn't heard from me in twenty-four hours.

Jennifer(TEXT): Okay, Pru. You've either been kidnapped or are having a marathon fuckfest, but either way, you need to call me back.

Most of my notifications were from Daddy. I opened up the latest voicemail and put it on speaker: "Hey, honey bear, it's Daddy. I haven't heard from you in a few days, and I know you aren't happy with the amenities at the new apartment, but I'm sure I can get you out of the lease if you're really upset. I'm going to Dallas on Wednesday, but I'll transfer your allowance before I go. Call me back. Love you."

The next message started before I could stop it, and my mother's abrasive vibrato echoed around the bathroom: "Prudence. It's Mom. I'm up in Napa for the week with James. Have you heard from your father? Of course you have. You're probably off somewhere with him and Julie. Well, I hope you and your new gal pal are spending all his money somewhere. The gold-digging floozy better do it now before he dumps her for the next bimbo in a short skirt. Did you know I saw your father flirting with your Uncle Blake's secretary just last week? Anyway, a story for another time. I'll call you when I get home from Napa. Kisses."

If I rolled my eyes any harder, they'd fall out of my head. Instead of calling either of my parents, I called Jennifer, and she answered on the first ring.

"Oh my God, Pru, where have you been!" she shrieked. "I've been worried sick!"

"You're not going to believe this," I whispered. "I went home with Ezra St. Croix."

"Shut. Up."

"I'm in his bathroom right now."

"Oh my fucking God. Tell me everything." She sounded breathless.

"I can't right now but I'll tell you one thing. The rumors are true. He is incredible in bed and his cock is pierced. No man will ever live up to this weekend." I swooned, and my stomach knotted at the idea that this time with Ezra was only a fling.

"Take pictures." She laughed and hung up.

I shoved my phone back into my purse. The battery was low and I needed to save the last of the charge to call a taxi downstairs. I finished primping and fluffing my hair before going back into the bedroom. Ezra was pulling a shirt over his head, his lean stomach rippling as the crisp white T-shirt covered his torso.

"You're staring again." The smug, sexy smile on his face said he wasn't at all bothered.

"Guilty."

I smiled up at him as he pulled me into his arms

for a soft, sweet kiss. His hand wrapped around my chin, bringing me up to my tiptoes.

"Time for me to go, beautiful."

My lips turned down in an instant.

His thumb pulled at the edge of my pout and his tongue glided across my flesh. "You should be here when I get back."

That invitation had my ears and heart perked. "Really?"

His hooded eyes watched his finger trace over my mouth then traveled up to meet mine. "Unless you're sick of me already."

"How long will you be gone?" I was aware that I was sounding clingy, but I couldn't live here for a month waiting for him to come back from wherever he was going.

"A couple days. I owe someone a favor." His warm breath against my cheek felt like silk. How could he just leave?

"Let me come with you." I wasn't asking. Something in my chest was screaming at me to not let him go alone.

Maybe I was scared that he would forget about me if I was out of his sight for that long, but there was something nagging at my core that didn't want me to be too far away from him.

"Not this time." He stepped away and headed to the bathroom vanity. "I want you here, missing me."

He looked at me through the mirror as he combed gel through his hair.

"It'll be quicker if I go alone." He moved on to smudging black liner around his eyes, making them look almost white instead of crystal blue.

"You're going to go see another woman, aren't you?"

His mouth formed an open, sarcastic smile. I may have been overreacting, but he wasn't denying it.

"I'm not going to stay here while you're fucking someone else a hundred miles away." I placed my hands on my cocked hips and gave him my most practiced death stare. "Take me with you."

"You're lucky I have to leave or else I'd fuck that attitude right out of you." He slipped past me and walked out into the living room to grab his keys and a helmet.

"Ezra." I used his name as a warning and waited for him to mull over his next rebuttal.

He looked me up and down then looked at his helmet.

I gave him a look that said I wasn't budging and that I was willing to drag this out for longer than he was willing to deal with.

"Fuck." He growled, annoyed but defeated. "Fine."

My stomach flipped with my victory, but I didn't let him see it fully affect me.

He crossed the room and pulled me into his torso and took a handful of my backside with a hard smack. "But I have half a mind to redden your ass before I put you on my bike."

I squirmed in his hold, but he had a firm grip. His cock pressed into my hip and my thighs clenched. I'd never been so sore, but the way he was looking at me with his signature smolder made my pussy ache.

This man could use me for the rest of my life and it wouldn't be enough.

After we stopped at his brother's apartment for a second helmet, we headed to my place so I could pack an overnight bag and change into something more comfortable for the ride.

Ezra lurking around my new apartment felt almost sweet, like he wanted to know more about me without having to ask. When I came out of my room with my leather travel bag on my back, he was holding a photo of my father and me standing outside of Stanford on the day of my graduation.

"What did you study?" He sounded melancholy.

"Business. I got my MBA a few months ago. Daddy has been carving out a position for me at Solar Star, his international solar development company. I know everyone who works there because he's owned it since I was in middle school. Everyone still sees me as some brace-faced kid. But until then, I'm enjoying life and going where the universe takes me."

He stood silent a moment more then said, "The universe is unpredictable."

"Isn't that exciting?"

"Riveting." His lip curled with his sarcastic response.

I pulled at his arm, and we finally left.

It isn't that I didn't want Ezra to know me, but the truth was, I didn't have the drive or desire to work at my father's constantly changing business. I knew working for Daddy would be easy and I'd get to live in L.A. again. San Jose was not my vibe. But I wasn't ready to give up the parties and the freedom I had in college.

When we got back down to Ezra's bike, he swung his leg over it and took a seat. The bike sank under his weight, but he didn't put his helmet on right away. He shook out his raven hair, squinting in the sun high above.

He was breathtaking. His black hair shined as he raked his fingers through it. The tattoos on his neck ticked with the tightening of the column of his throat. The snag of shadows under the sharp angles of his cheekbones and chin made him look as if he had been sculpted by God himself.

"Ready?"

That soul-melting smile sent heat to my cheeks and longing to my chest. My answer was my arms around his shoulders and a kiss intended to make him crave more.

He cursed under his breath when I finally pulled away. Then, I put on my helmet and slipped onto the seat behind him. He adjusted the situation I'd created in his pants then pulled his own helmet on.

I clung to him for dear life until we reached a less traffic-dense stretch of freeway. The ocean peeked in and out of view from the hills and valleys down the I-5 as Ezra swerved and maneuvered the motorcycle between slower vehicles. With each loud rev of the engine, I hugged his torso tighter until I was practically wearing his leather jacket.

Down a long straight, Ezra lifted his hands above his head and allowed the bike to drift long enough for my screams of terror to echo in my helmet. My nails clawed into his chest and my life was flashing before my eyes.

The wind carried his laugh back to me. He gripped the handles again and hit the gas to bring one last scream from my throat.

"Don't worry, beautiful," he yelled over the noise of the road. "I'll take care of you."

The asshole.

My thighs squeezed against him, and a wicked idea took form.

I slipped my hand beneath the front of his shirt to the soft, taut skin of his stomach. The hair leading down to his waistband parted with my fingers. I didn't have to struggle to go any farther; his cock was thick and waiting for me to take hold of it. The spaces between his piercings were just wide enough for my fingers at this angle.

Next, I shifted my hips forward and circled my pelvis against his lower back. The friction was warm but not nearly enough to get me off. Still, my point was made.

A deep groan vibrated his back, and his hips gave a gentle buck, but I didn't move my arm to stroke him. If he was going to tease me, I would give him a dose of my own version of thrilling medicine.

I pulsed my grip on his cock, and he throbbed in response. My free hand trailed up to his chest and I dragged my nails slowly down. He let out a loud and devious curse. I wanted him desperately, but the power I was wielding was heady and dazing. He was at my mercy and I was going to savor every minute.

Ezra brought a hand down from the handlebars to cup my knuckles. He wanted me to add pressure, for me to move, but I held firm. His frustration was growing, and the more he searched for release, the more my body wound up.

Would it be possible to climax from the sheer anticipation of him punishing me later?

I didn't have a chance to find out. The horn of a semitruck blared behind us, and Ezra hit the gas. I clutched his waist as he veered into the far lane to allow the impatient driver to pass. We came to a skidding stop on the side of the road on a small patch of gravel, and I leaped off the back of the bike and straight into a panic attack.

My heart was pounding in my chest, and I ripped off my helmet to gasp for air. Ezra pulled his own helmet off, swung his leg over the seat, and swept me up into his arms. His mouth crashed over mine in a hard, demanding kiss. I wrapped my legs around his waist and my arms around his heaving shoulders. He pulled my hips down onto him, his hard cock pressed roughly to my center through my jeans.

"Do you see what you do to me?" he gruffed,

only taking his lips away long enough to get the words out.

Our tongues coaxed, tasted, and filled each other's greedy mouths. The life-or-death moment didn't dampen his hunger, and something about that made me feel invincible.

He set me on my feet, but when our eyes met, he had a fierce determination on his face. With his hands on my waist, he walked me back until my calves hit the low metal guardrail.

His fingers worked the button of my pants, and his husky voice rose over the roar of passing cars. "This is what you wanted, right?"

I nodded, not taking my gaze away from his. I thought I knew what I wanted when I started playing with him, but the unhinged look of need in his eyes was more than I had bargained for.

His tongue slowly wet his lips as he tugged down the waistband of my pants to reveal just skin. No underwear to slow him down. His hunger turned to rabid starvation.

"Turn around."

I did as I was told and curled my fingers around the biting edge of the metal railing. The drop into the valley below was steep and ended in dry, stripped bushes. I braced myself the best I could and focused on the words Ezra had said earlier.

I'll take care of you.

The cool air on my ass and pussy didn't last long.

"Now scream for me." Ezra lined up the head of his cock at my entrance and slammed inside.

My lungs constricted, and my voice burst out. He pulled his hips back and plunged into my needy cunt. The tension low in my belly wound tight as he filled me and withdrew again and again.

His fingers gripped my hips and held me in place for every brutal thrust. My jeans around my knees acted like a brace to keep me somewhat upright, and the sound of my nails scraping the guardrail gave me goose bumps, but I held on for dear life.

Ezra thrust harder. The deep throb of my walls around him sent me over the peak, and I crashed into an intense orgasm. My moan echoed down the ridge below and was followed by Ezra's.

"Oh fuck, baby," he bellowed and pulled out of me in time to spill over the ground next to my feet.

He gave himself a few last pumps, and I scrambled to pull my pants up over my convulsing pussy. I slumped to my knees to catch my breath, and he stretched his arms over his head, somehow already zipped up and able to stand.

My legs trembled, but air had finally filled my lungs comfortably.

Ezra leaned down and, with a gentle pull of my chin, kissed me softly. "Back on the bike, beautiful."

8
GAAP

P ru tagging along hadn't been part of the plan. I couldn't guarantee that the spell Eli had given me would mask my influence and ownership of her. Not to mention that I wasn't sure how I was going to shield her from the fact that I was a prince of Hell going to pay a visit to a colossal beast hidden within a Catholic priest.

She may as well claim insanity now before attempting to cut off my balls.

I'd called ahead to a hotel nearby, but we went straight to the little white mission church in La Jolla. It was positioned on the corner of a busy block, less than a mile from the beach. If you blinked while passing, you'd miss it.

I pulled into one of the few parking spots in front of the brick wall and iron gate, then I waited for Pru to dismount before hopping off myself.

"A church?" She scoffed. "We drove three hours for Monday Mass?"

"Stay by the bike," I said harsher than I intended, but it shut her up.

The conversation with the Leviathan would be short. Unlike my brethren, who resided in Heaven, or the Fallen, the Leviathan toed the line between beast and higher being. Many of his depictions through the ages were those of a monstrous sea serpent. In others, he was seen as a god himself.

In this century, he was posing as a Catholic priest. It was well known that if a demon possessed a human host, the vessel wouldn't last long. Human bodies were not made to contain our power. The perk of being made into a creature outside of humanity, demon, or angel was that the Leviathan would inhabit a human for whole lifetimes at a time.

Through the iron gate, an older, scruffy man dressed in priest's robes and donning a warm, inviting grin stood just outside the main entrance. The church lawn was only a few yards long, but he likely felt me, rather than heard my bike approaching.

"A prince of Hell has come to confess his sins," he said and peered over my shoulder. "Is she your offering?"

I chuckled, but beneath the humor was a bite of ire. Trying my best to hide it, I took the three steps up to him in one reach of my legs and embraced the Leviathan.

"It's good to see you too, mighty beast."

"Come, come! We have so much to talk about."

He clapped my shoulder and led me into the sanctuary. Stained-glass murals dashed vivid colors over the dark-red carpets that led to the steps of the main altar.

I jumped right to the point. "What do you know about a copper ring that Lucifer holds dear?"

This didn't seem to catch him off guard.

He quirked a brow at me. "The ring that was taken from him by one of your own?"

"I don't know about that, but I don't doubt that you're right."

He moved away from the accusation and clasped his hands behind his back as I followed him up the wide aisle between the pews. "It's for healing, but it comes with a grave price. Like all of His most precious things."

"*The Lord gave and the Lord has taken away.*" I recited the human scripture.

"Funny like that, our Father."

The Leviathan knew better than any of us how cruel our Father could be. He had been created with his companion for sport, but when it became too much of a risk to the humans if he and his mate bred, He took the other half of the

Leviathan's existence away without another thought.

"How can I find the ring?" I asked. "Ipos has been unable to locate it."

He tilted his head at me—reminiscent of the inhuman being living within this vessel—then down the aisle from where we'd come. It would have been easy for a human to brush off his odd behaviors as mannerisms from someone who had dedicated their life to God.

"She doesn't have anything to do with this scavenger hunt, and yet you brought her with you. Why?"

"Boredom," I lied simply.

He laughed to himself and shook his head. "Spoken so truly as one of His most lost sons." My lip ticked with annoyance at this comment. "Come back tomorrow morning. I have an old tracking spell that might assist your brother in his pursuit. But be warned, the user of the ring will suffer greatly if their intentions aren't pure of heart."

I scoffed. "No such thing."

He shrugged and gave me an amused *hmm*. "That isn't for us to determine."

Spoken like a true neutral being.

I couldn't help but search for the sea serpent lurking below the wrinkled and sun-stained skin of the human exterior before me. He'd mastered the illusion of his current occupation and status among the mortal sheep he shepherded. An all-knowing wolf leading the flock.

"If you change your mind about your new companion, I could find a place for her to kneel."

My cutting glance sent him into a fit of laughter that accompanied me on my way out of the church.

Mad bastard.

9

PRU

It was too hot to stand in the sun while Ezra was inside talking to his priest. I retreated to the shade under a tall pine tree in the court-yard. The breeze from the ocean, which was only a few blocks away, was cool enough to send goose bumps up my arms.

The church was cute: a white adobe exterior with gorgeous stained-glass windows. A low brick wall boxed in the entrance and housed several statues. One of them was a depiction of Michael slaying Lucifer. The archangel looked almost like a child standing over a half-dragon, half-man with his face screwed up in anger and hatred.

I never would have guessed that Ezra was reli-gious or attached to this small Catholic church in San Diego. Perhaps he was giving a confession or whatever. Wasn't that what Catholics did?

"Hello there, can I help you?"

I jumped at the question and the sudden appearance of a man walking across the lawn toward me from a side door.

"Uh . . . no, I'm waiting for someone," I said, straightening the hem of my shirt. It had been riding up my stomach.

"Aren't we all," he replied with a warm, ironic smile.

"Right." I looked over to the doorway then back to Ezra's motorcycle, unsure which direction to retreat to.

The man was unbothered by my darting eyes. He was dressed in all-black clerical clothing. The white collar around his neck marked him as a priest, but the line of sweat disappearing behind it made my throat tighten.

"Are you new to the church?" he asked.

"Yes, but I'm visiting with a friend."

He looked around, and his eyes snagged on the motorcycle before meeting my gaze again. "You must be very good friends if you've come to church with them."

I nodded, wishing that Ezra would come outside and save me from explaining to this man of God that I was a nonbeliever.

"It takes a special connection to embrace each other's faith," he continued and made another short step closer. "I've lost many friends in my path to God. I commend you for your bravery."

"I'm just here for moral support." My comment was more of an invitation for him to leave, but I had a feeling he hadn't accepted it.

"Moral support," he repeated, dragging the words over his tongue and through his teeth. "Wonderful."

"Thanks." I made to take a step around him, but he shifted into my path.

"If you were to join us for worship, I could guarantee it would open your eyes to great truths."

I took a step back. His casual tone was gone, and the severity in his eyes dug down into my gut.

"Truths about God?" I asked, clarifying that he was still only trying to shove his religion down my throat and not a gag.

"There are many fallacies about the temptations of others. Sometimes, it takes the support of strangers to rid yourself of those indulgences. The holy always overpower the wicked."

Was he slut-shaming me in a church courtyard?

I internally screamed harder for Ezra. For him to walk down the steps and whisk me away to wickedly overpower me in our hotel room, far away from this creep.

"Thank you for the invitation," I said, "but I think I should go find my friend."

"All are welcome. Truth can penetrate even the darkest souls."

With that unnerving statement and a perk of his brow, he turned around and disappeared around the corner, leaving me frozen in place. My stomach hollowed and I had the distinct impulse to run—fast and far. If only I could get my feet to move.

"Pru." Ezra's voice sounded dangerous as he emerged from the church moments too late and crossed the short distance to me.

His patch-covered jacket engulfed my vision and pushed away the blinding white gleam of the church walls. When his hands clamped around my arms and pulled me even closer, I felt the harsh anger coming from him, but it didn't feel directed toward me.

"I told you to stay by the bike." He looked around us, and the hardness of a man ready to bring death down on someone's head was heavy in his eyes. "Where did he go?"

"Wha—where did who go?" My brows furrowed as I looked up at him.

"The priest. Where did that weasel skulk off to?" He bent his head to meet my confused gaze, and I pointed in the vague direction that the man had gone. Ezra whipped his head around to look then turned back to me. "We should go."

"But—"

"Now."

I didn't attempt to argue further and didn't have much of an option. Ezra took hold of my wrist and pulled me out of the courtyard to his motorcycle.

⚜

Ezra didn't say more than two words to me until we were checked into the hotel and setting our overnight bags on the crisp white sheets.

"What did he say to you?" His voice still carried a harsh worry that felt foreign to the charismatic man who'd seemed fearless.

"Why?" I sprawled out on the bed and flung my arms over my head. "What could that stranger have said to me in the brief moment you left me outside that's made you so curious?"

For a moment, I had mistaken his interest for jealousy. He had, after all, bashed in a man's skull at The Deacon for looking up my dress.

But now, the more his mood shifted, the less I understood his intentions.

He refused to meet my eyes. "You don't understand how intrusive strangers can be for someone like me."

"That's why you didn't want me to come with

you. You didn't want to be seen with someone normal."

I knew that wasn't the truth, but he would either lie to agree or he would come out with what was really eating at him.

The edge of the bed sank under the weight of his knee, and he pulled his body over me until his lips grazed mine.

"I'm not playing games with you," he said in a heated warning. My breath hung on his every word. "If I tell you something is important, you have to trust that it is and listen."

Not an explanation or what I needed to hear to want to end this argument.

If I had to drag the truth about this trip and his odd behavior out of him kicking and screaming, I was ready to do so.

I pushed up on his shoulder, and he rolled onto his side to allow me to get to my feet. I rounded on him.

"I'm not some roadie slut who is going to go along with everything you say without thinking for themselves." The venom in my voice was heavy on my tongue. "You're acting weird. Scared. What are we doing here, Ezra? Why are you so freaked out over some random creep in a churchyard?"

I spread my arms wide for dramatics. The heat of the argument had started to rise in my chest and was spurred on by the vacant look on his face. We'd spent most of our time together naked and testing our physical limits. But for the first time, I was showing him that I had real fight in me—apart from the sassy mouth he loved to fuck.

"Tell me what's going on. The truth," I demanded, my arms crossed and hip cocked.

He sat up and braced his elbows on his knees, his face buried in his hands. For a moment, I saw a crack in his exterior, but then the bare skin between the inked flesh of his neck and shoulders turned red.

Anger.

He was furious.

"I owe one of my brothers a favor and had to visit an old friend to fulfill that obligation. You didn't have to be here. In fact, I insisted that you stay at the apartment and wait for me to come back, but you wanted to come with me, like a clingy *roadie slut* you turn your nose up at. If either of us should be explaining ourselves, it's you. Why are you so secretive? What don't you want me to know?"

He'd lost it.

Wherever this paranoia came from, it was centered around the church and the mysterious favor he owed his brother.

I couldn't stop the tears from forming in my eyes. I always cried when I was angry, and it was my most annoying fault. It made whoever my opponent was think I was weak or about to fold.

Unfortunately for Ezra, I was not so easily beaten.

The harsh lines of his rage softened a little, and he held out a hand to comfort me. His fingers brushed my skin, but I whipped around to face the door.

"Don't touch me," I said, annoyance budding in my tone. "I wanted to come, but I would have stayed if I knew you were going to turn into this lunatic."

"You don't understand. You couldn't." He sounded tired or indifferent, and the latter sent ice into my belly.

I wiped the tears from my cheeks then looked over my shoulder at him. "Try me."

He sighed, heavy and almost broken. He was holding back still, and it was clear that he wasn't going to trust me. The illusion that we could become something more, that he had seen me as more than just a good lay, was shattered. The humiliation hit me, and the tears gathering on my lashes were full of real pain.

I'd been nothing and would only ever be nothing to Ezra St. Croix.

Rock star. Playboy. Heartbreaker.

The inner scolding pounded against my eardrums as I gathered my few items and slammed the door behind me. I took off down the hall to the elevator and stood inside it before the last thread of hope snapped.

I held the doors open.

One.

Two.

Breathe, Pru. He'll follow. He has to follow you.

Four.

Five.

He can't be this cruel.

Seven.

Eight.

Just one more second. He'll come running.

Ten.

I let go of the button.

The doors closed, and my heart broke.

10
GAAP

I paced the floor of our room for hours, waiting for her to come back. It became clear that I was going to have to find her and drag her back myself. When I reached out with the delicate connection I had to her soul, I came back empty-handed. I couldn't get a clear read on which direction she'd gone.

When I got down to my bike, I could only feel her breathing. She was asleep somewhere, probably in another hotel or close by. I rode up and down several blocks but again, there wasn't a clear indication of her whereabouts. Until she woke up, I would have to wait and stew in the fury building inside of me. For the remainder of the night, I tossed and turned until I reluctantly slept.

When the early morning came, and I couldn't take being in the hotel any longer, I headed to the church to meet with the Leviathan. My only company on the ride was the nervous energy mixed with the sick feeling in my stomach that something wasn't right. Her soul was still within the city limits, and she was somewhere dark and still not fully awake. If I couldn't pinpoint a location, I couldn't step through the void to her side. I would have to call in reinforcements if she didn't turn up after I met with the Leviathan. If Eli was still hanging around The Deacon, he could assist me.

The small semblance of a plan didn't rid my gut of the knots that had been coiled there since she'd walked out of the hotel room. I had let my anger get the better of me. The secret of who I really was and trying to shield her from a world she would never be able to unsee had thickened my head and caused me to push her away.

If something had happened to her, it was my fault. If she found her way back home and rejected me when I finally did find her, she would be entitled. Both scenarios were punishments I deserved. I hadn't taken a human companion in ages. I'd gotten too attached to the last one, and he'd ended up dying from the party lifestyle I had introduced him to. His loss had been devastating and was partly why I had given up my crown and responsibilities.

I had long since healed, but allowing myself to become infatuated with any being since, then had been too painful. Humans, especially, were fragile and easily lost. Enduring a prince of Hell was brutal on their bodies and minds, but Pru was different. Our first night together had woken a hunger in me that only she could tame. She'd lasted longer in my bed than most and still wanted more. I'd picked her out of convenience, but I was questioning what my brothers had seen so blatantly. Would I really have been able to use Pru as a barrier from Alessio?

I had to find her. Find a way to keep her. I needed her.

The church parking lot was empty when I pulled up on my bike. It was still early, and the smoggy air that hung over the mountainous horizon burned with the cresting sun.

I didn't know if The Leviathan would be in the sanctuary yet—he likely lived in a dwelling nearby—but I would wait at the steps if I had to. When I approached the angular archway, one of the doors was slightly ajar, and a dim light flickered inside. It set my nerves on edge, and my spine straightened as I reached out a hand to push it open.

My head was pounding, and my eyes felt like they were swollen shut. The splitting pain at the crown of my head pulsed, and if I wasn't bleeding, I knew I would be bruised.

Broken memories from the night before flashed in and out of focus with the waning of lights and spots over my blurred vision. I'd been screaming for Ezra in a small, cramped place for what seemed like hours. I had either passed out from panic, pain, or exhaustion, and I didn't remember being moved.

After Ezra had let me walk out of the hotel, I made it to the end of the block before I fell to my knees on the sidewalk.

A man had stopped and crouched down next to me. "Are you all right, miss?" His voice was low and familiar, but I couldn't place it.

"No. I'm an idiot," I'd sobbed. "And now I have to find my way back home tonight. I shouldn't have come down here."

I hiccuped through my jumbled word vomit to the stranger. He brushed a hand down my back and shushed me softly.

"There's a coffee shop around the corner. Let me buy you a coffee while you figure out your next move."

His offer was kind. Kinder than most people would be to someone losing their ever-loving mind out in public.

I'd shaken my head and got to my feet. "Thank you, but . . ."

When I looked up at the man, I realized it was the priest I'd met in the courtyard. The one who had caused the fight between Ezra and me.

I had a choice to make: run away from the man and back up to Ezra or allow the man to buy me coffee and maybe get answers from him.

Neither felt right in my stomach, but I was reeling from the argument with Ezra, and I couldn't cry on the sidewalk all night.

The last thing I remembered was rounding the corner with the man and looking for the coffee shop he'd said was close by. Then, everything went black and my memories were broken up by my own screams for help and missing time.

Now, I was finally peeling open my eyelids to focus on the room around me. The cloudy early-morning light was streaming in from colorful glass windows. The smell of burning candles and dim dots of light deepened my suspicion that I was somewhere sinister.

The pain in my head radiated down to my face, and when I tried to wipe the grogginess from my eyes to get a better look, I couldn't raise my arm. My wrists, torso, and ankles were tied to a hard wooden chair. My pelvis was aching from it, adding to the onslaught of agony assaulting my groggy brain.

The room was vast and open, but my vision was fading out again. Pain had taken over my senses. My eyes drifted shut until a hard smack set fire to my cheek. I tried to scream, but it was muffled by something tight over my lips.

An icy splash of water rushed over my body and up my nose. My eyes bolted open and searched for whoever was trying to drown me.

"Time to wake up. He'll be looking for you," said a cold voice. "For that to be possible, you have to be conscious."

I turned one way, then the other, but I couldn't see the source of the disembodied voice.

"In my experience, a desperate demon is a careless demon. He'll be worried sick about his precious Prudence."

This man knew me. He knew my full first name. Was he talking about Ezra?

How would Ezra know how to find me, and was this man calling him a demon because of the kind of music he performed?

He had to be some sort of nut-job-stalker-Jesus-freak hell-bent on ridding the world of the plague of good music and fun. He definitely had to be crazy, but that didn't change the fact that he had me strapped to a chair and had bashed me over the head. The slap across my face had woken me up, but the freezing water had brought my fight-or-flight instincts to the surface.

The few steps down from the altar would be enough to break the chair if I landed just right. Then I could run out the door or use scraps of the chair as a weapon. But before I could coil my muscles to make the small leap over the edge, his hands gripped the back of the chair. He leaned down once more to deliver a sentence that set my heart slamming against my ribcage with a new kind of fear.

"He's here."

12
GAAP

Silent dread filled up the small church. The iron smell of blood and the salt of tears flared my nostrils before my eyes adjusted to the candlelight and darkened sanctuary. The previous glory was dimmed by the evil being committed within.

My stomach sank when I realized the small, wet figure bound to a chair on the altar was Pru. Silver bands of duct tape made an excessive X over her lips, and her tear-stained cheeks were red. My focus landed on the distinct mark of finger outlines just between the frayed tape.

I tamped down the inferno blazing inside of me. Alessio was nowhere to be seen, but the plea in Pru's eyes told me he was close.

"This has gone too far, Alessio," I called out while I panned the pews for movement.

Several rows up, a dark shadow emerged. His short dark hair was dashed with early grey. Chasing the damned had aged him. Though he was of average height, his thin body made him look taller. His scarred hands passed over the tops of the pews as he walked, and the etchings on his skin were fiery red from the hellfire he'd used to make them.

"Who tells your kind when you've gone too far? When you've corrupted entire generations of human hearts and triggered the end of days?" He spoke softly as he reached the middle aisle.

There was no urgency in his tone while he lingered in the path between Pru and me. He was too confidently reserved. Not at all like I had thought he would be after the mortal crimes he'd committed to get me in his clutches.

"Are we in the end of days again?" I joked. "It's been a while since the last time the world was said to be ending. I don't suppose you have an ancient calendar or tablet from a long-dead prophet hidden in your robes?"

He turned his back to me and strode to the dias then took the three steps up the platform to stand by Pru's side.

"I don't need false prophecies to tell me what I can see all around us. The Leviathan posing as a holy leader is proof enough that the wicked have become too powerful."

It was a common sophism among men of the cloth. One that Alessio's mentor had spread like wildfire while he'd conducted hundreds of exorcisms in his time. Before him, there'd been dogma that spoke of the end of days for humankind at the hands of Lucifer and his followers. But those days had all come and gone. The same as Alessio's would. The same as whoever came after. Human minds could not fathom the infinity of forever, so they took their grain of history as the way things always had been and always would be.

"Fighting all the big, bad evil on your own?" I looked around him mockingly but noted where he would likely try to escape when it was time for me to strike. "No angel willing to assist you on your crusade? My brother Auriel must be too busy to send a lesser angel to your side in your darkest hour."

This battle Alessio's brotherhood had fought for centuries had never been endorsed by our Father or the archangels. A greener soldier may have aided here and there through the ages, but never without a long timeout in Heaven. Mikael was the most recent to be reprimanded, as the rumors were told. He'd stuck his nose where it didn't belong and had gotten one of Father's golden children killed.

"I have dedicated my life to hunting your kind," Alessio said. "To fight a war that was laid at my feet by those who could never and would never defeat evil. I fight for the Father on a mortal mission."

"A fool's errand," I corrected him. "The separation between the Fallen and our holy brothers was done by His hand. What makes us evil for wanting what He so freely gave to you?"

"That's poetic coming from the prince of Hell whose purpose is to deter man from righteousness and lead them down the path of ruin."

I couldn't hide the snide smile his words brought to my lips. "Laze does not make an apostate."

He huffed with a mixture of disdain and sardonic humor then circled behind the bait he'd intended to use to lure me inside. Pride sparked in his eyes at his own vain cleverness.

Pru wriggled against her restraints, and her muffled whimper through the tape sent fire through my blood. She was mine. If anyone was going to tie her to a chair and cause tears to stream down her perfectly flushed cheeks, it would be me.

"You'd argue it was free will though, wouldn't you. Free will for humans to make their own mistakes. Commit their own sins and submit their souls to you." He leaned down closer to my Pru. "Like this one has. She's very committed to you, demon prince. Screamed your false name for hours until her voice was hoarse. I tried to tell her that you'd never be able to hear her. The wards I marked on her skin silenced the bond you forced upon her. That seemed to be news to your plaything. Didn't you mention that her soul bore your tainted mark?"

He cocked his head at Pru, but her eyes were fixed on me. Her face was full of regret and pleas for salvation. His thumb wiped a tear roughly from her chin and brought it to his lips, then he darted his tongue out and hissed as if it were acid.

"Putrid harlot," he spat over her. "Gave over her soul to you in a fit of lust. Damnation eternal is all that awaits her now. That's all her prince can provide."

Each of his determined breaths became an agitation and insult as anger pounded in my ears. The false cool shell I'd been holding on to was cracking with every pump of blood through his veins. He was testing the wrong demon. I had my freedom to live on Earth to lose, but if he touched Pru once more, I was going to take him with me into fiery oblivion.

"Pru, look at me." I was internally reeling from my explosive rage but spoke softly to her. "I'm going to get you out of here. What did I promise you?"

Her glassy eyes bulged and spilled a renewed stream of hot tears. She shook her head, and the desperation on her face sent a piercing pain through my chest.

I'll take care of you.

"Neither one of you will be leaving this church

113

intact, Gaap." Alessio scoffed. "You may have abdicated your throne, but you wouldn't bring war down on your brothers. Running from me for so long has proved that pacts among devils are stronger than my predecessors had recorded."

I glowered. "Starting a war over a woman isn't unheard of."

"How have those wars ended? Killing me would bring more than just war. It would give rise to the slaughter of all demons on Earth. You'd be breaking the agreement Lucifer made with the Order, which would call every angel on high down on your heads. And I've heard through the grapevine that they have been itching for a fight since one of their own was murdered in the name of love all too recently."

His upper lip curled into a disgusted grimace. He was enjoying taunting me and was underestimating the Fallen. Clearly, my brothers doing anything pure by human definition was unheard of in his circles.

I returned his cruel smile. "What would a priest know of love? You pine for a connection to a Father you have never met and are instructed to worship without question."

Alessio De Santis was far from the holy man he made himself out to be. No man could commit his life to hunting down my kind and not get his hands covered in the blood of the innocent. His treatment of Pru was enough of a reason to send his soul to

Hell to burn for all eternity at the hands of my legions.

Alessio reached into a fold of his priest robes and pulled out a thick, disheveled book. The black leather was worn and ripped on the spine, and no title or author name was visible. My eyes fixed on it, but not for the reason he assumed. I could hear a low ringing coming from its pages—something pure as sunlight and just as destructive.

That book was leaving this church with Pru and me. I owed Eli a debt, and I intended to fulfill it.

"Your concern for my relationship with God is touching, but I am through with your games, Prince of Sloth."

My heart raced as he began chanting his incantations in the tongue of his brotherhood. The repetitive phrases felt like sledgehammers against my eardrums. Muscle and cartilage tore from my bones. My spine cracked. I could feel the ripping of my immortal soul from my earthly form.

I had to get to her. She had to run far away without looking back. Alessio wasn't going to allow her to breathe after my mortal body had melted away and my demonic presence on this plane had disappeared as if I'd never existed.

My fingernails dug into the aged brown grout between the smooth tiles, and I pulled myself across the floor. Before my hand could reach her, Alessio became a blockade.

He started another line of his passages. His voice echoed around the high ceilings, his vibrato climbing.

My nose began to bleed. My blood vessels filled to their limits as my soul searched for a way out of every cell.

The last of my existence on this plane was coming to an end, and the most damning part was having to watch Pru's face contort as she screamed through the tape.

I felt her calling for me to stay. To fight.

My vision went black, and I waited for the pain to fall away, for Alessio's voice to fade, but it didn't.

One moment, he was reciting his hymns. The next, he was shouting in pain.

I felt my strength return as the sounds of a scuffle replaced his spellcasting and the cracking of my limbs. A wave of heat came from my left. A body slammed onto the ground to my right.

"Ezra." Pru's frantic voice perked my ears, and her hands framed my face. "Ezra, please wake up. Fuck. Look at me, please."

I could hear the tears tightening her throat and feel the trembling in her fingers as she swept damp strands of hair from my forehead.

"Don't cry, beautiful," I croaked.

Each draw of breath strained my ribs and the tendons that were knitting themselves back into place. The process of being put back together was just as painful as it was to be broken.

When I pried my lids open to check that Pru was intact, I was met with the wreckage around us. She'd thrown herself from the old chair and used one of the shards of wood to impale Alessio. He was lying in a pool of his own blood. The death rattle from his lungs marked the time he had left.

The heat licking at my exposed skin was coming from a fire set by candles that had been tipped over as Pru saved my life. Flames were climbing the altar cloths and pouring over the printed sermon that had been laid out for the next service. As soon as the heat felt as if it were going to get out of hand, an alarm began to ring through the church and water sprayed from the sprinklers above.

"The book." I looked over the ground around us for the payment I owed. Though the spell Eli had placed on me hadn't worked on my connection to Pru, I knew it needed to be taken after experiencing the power the book held in the hands of a Hunter.

I sat up and rolled onto my hands and knees to feel around the floor, over debris and through bloody water, for the blasted tome that had almost torn my soul from Earth.

"We have to go. Fuck the book." Pru's panicked

voice echoed in my head as she pulled at my shoulder.

Her clothes were soaked, and the dark stains of my blood on her blouse were spreading and running. She'd just attempted to murder another human. It was self-defense, but she'd already followed her fight reflex, and now flight was taking hold.

"I need that book." I grunted, holding my sore side where ribs had been shattered. "I can't let him leave with it."

She spun in place. Her eyes scanned the dais, then she bent low.

"Here." She shoved the book into my outstretched hand.

It was dripping red from the puddle of diluted blood it had been lying in. I yelped in pain and let go, and a loud thud came from where I'd let it fall. The wretched thing had been warded against demons. My skin where I had made contact looked as if I'd dunked it in boiling acid.

Pru gasped and knelt at my side. "What the fuck, Ezra?"

"I'll be fine. Grab the book and let's go." I finally got to my feet and stumbled down the steps to the aisle.

I leaned on the first pew to support my broken body while my limbs righted themselves, finally giving me stability. Stabbing pain filled my gut and extremities as nerves grew back from where they had been severed. The perk of once being holy was that I would heal rapidly. Another hour and this would all be a sick nightmare, and I would be back to my full power.

"Where did he go?" Pru asked.

I cursed and peered through the spray of water coming from above but could hardly see Pru, who was only an arm's length away.

"I don't know, but I can't protect us here," I said, struggling to inhale without collapsing from pain. "Pru, please."

I held out my arm, and she looked back to where Alessio had been sprawled out. After a long, contemplative pause, she tucked into my side and helped me walk out to the front archway.

Alessio seemed to have been close to death, but not nearly close enough. And if he truly did manage to live to see another day, it would be a new game of cat and church mouse.

13
PRU

I'd killed someone.
Hadn't I?
I didn't feel guilty.

Did that make me a bad person? Ezra didn't seem to think so, or at least he didn't seem to acknowledge that it was a reality.

We made it outside and onto Ezra's motorcycle before the police and fire department showed up. I'd never know how he'd managed to drive us back to the hotel, but he was walking upright by the time we'd made it to his room.

"I owe you an explanation," he said, pulling off his wet clothes and letting them fall to the floor.

In nothing but his boxer briefs, he took a step toward me. The bruises that had been dark purple were now merely shadows in the spaces between inked skin. I held up the book that I'd been holding on to for dear life. Immediately, he stopped.

"What is this?" My hands shook.

That crazy man had talked about demons, spells, and angels. I hadn't believed any of it until I saw Ezra on the floor of the church being bent into a pretzel by nothing but the priest's words.

"Was what he said true?" My voice cracked. I couldn't believe what I was asking. "Are you some kind of monster?"

How could that be possible?

"He's a very sick man." Ezra held his hands up. The dried blood from his nose and mouth had stained his skin inky black.

His demeanor was too calm. His arms had been twisted grotesquely, and his torso had looked battered and crushed, but he was now standing in front of me like it had never happened.

If my own hands weren't covered in blood, I would say I'd dreamed it.

"Don't you dare try to gaslight me, Ezra. Or should I be calling you Prince Gaap?"

His jaw clenched at the title the priest used. In the blink of an eye, his fingers wrapped around the column of my neck. "That name from your lips will only bring you pain. You couldn't even begin to understand the implications of my title to the human race."

He was deadly; I knew that.

The murderous look in his eyes had been terrifying, and it wasn't even directed at me. If it hadn't been for the book that I was clutching close to my chest, I believed Ezra would have torn the priest limb from limb without a second thought. And though the hand around my throat made my heart race, he had shown that he would have done unspeakable things to save my life.

I gave him a challenging smirk through my lashes. "If that's true, then why do I feel more powerful when I say it? Like it demands your surrender."

His eyes fell to my lips and his grip loosened, but he didn't step away. "Is that what you need from me, Pru? Surrender?"

I swallowed hard at that image. "I want the truth. I want to hear you say it and not make me sound like I've lost my mind."

His voice dipped and took my stomach with it. "You don't need to use my true name to get that."

The long pause between us was filled with anger, mistrust, and charged emotions that were sure to gain momentum. Only the sound of my heart beating and our shared breath filled the void between us.

"I am one of the princes of Hell. I've roamed this plane for thousands of years. I have seen things that would make you question everything and nothing all at once. The man who tried to take you from me has been hunting my kind and destroying us."

"Us?" I was trying so hard to suspend my disbelief and follow his explanation, but the new pieces of this puzzle were jagged in my foggy brain.

"Demons. The Fallen." He finally stepped away and took a pained breath. "My brothers."

"Why didn't you just kill him? If you're so powerful and your name should be feared, then why didn't you just destroy him before today?"

He glanced down at the book then back up at me. "There are a lot of reasons, but you're holding one. I needed that book to give to someone I owe a debt to."

I held it out in front of me like it would speak for itself. "Is this why we came down here?"

"No," he said simply. "I came to talk to an old friend who I suspect is somewhere in that church, slain. But I have no doubt that the book will still be valuable to whom I'm going to deliver it to. As for Alessio—the priest—it remains a mystery if he is still a danger without it."

A blurred moment came into focus. "You tricked me into giving you my soul?" I blurted. "You forced me into it, didn't you?"

"I need you." He cocked his head, and for the

first time, I saw a flicker of something inhuman in his eyes.

My spine straightened, and my skin went cold. "Why?"

"At first—" He took a step closer, and I held the book to my chest again, knowing it was the only weapon I had against him. "I needed a human shield to keep Alessio away from me."

The prickle of angry tears swelled behind my eyes. One fell to my cheek, and I cursed myself for allowing his words to hurt me.

"But then we spent that first night together." He looked down at his feet as if allowing me to cause him to feel emotions had defeated him. "I fought it as long as I could. I didn't plan on you becoming a weakness."

He took another step closer and cradled my jaw in his hands, bringing my chin up for our eyes to lock. His thumb swept away the shameful tear I'd shed.

"I didn't foresee you becoming my reason to fight for what I had been running from."

His lips brushed over mine, and the strength I'd been holding in my chest faltered. My adrenaline had saved our lives, and now that it was wearing off, I could feel the abuse my shoulder had taken when I landed on it.

I had been so sure I was going to be murdered

after having to watch Ezra die before my eyes, and having him standing in front of me, safe and whole, was bringing up more than complicated emotions.

He'd wanted to use me. But he hadn't been the only one running from responsibility in a life full of sex, freedom, and distractions. How long could we have outrun our paths?

And could we walk them together?

I didn't know the answer to either question or the dozens more running circles through my head. What I did know for sure was that when I finally allowed him to touch me well into the night, I melted into him and broke.

My body was in so much pain, but with my head on his chest, I could hear his heart beating and the tears came harder.

When I'd gotten free from that sadistic maniac and made it to his side, he was barely holding on. The beautiful clear blue of his eyes had turned to a stormy sea as the light dimmed. But when he heard me begging him to stay, he had. For me.

Was it more telling that he was willing to die for me or willing to survive?

14
GAAP

After we showered, I ordered room service. When I called Ipos, he confirmed that the Leviathan had been executed by Alessio. The local police were calling it a hate crime and a failed satanic ritual. More fear for the masses.

During the hours we'd spent baring our souls to one another, Pru told me more about her family. How her mother had used her as a pawn against her father in their divorce. Being the child of a socialite and a solar energy mogul had made her prey for the scum of Los Angeles.

"I was fourteen the first time I was given coke," she recounted. "By the time I turned eighteen, I'd already been to rehab twice. But it wasn't until I got into Stanford that I knew I needed to get my life together if I wanted to see graduation day. I've been clean and sober for six years now."

She'd been taken advantage of as a teen by B-list celebrities who'd kept her addicted to them by giving her booze and drugs. I added their names to a mental note to take care of later.

In exchange for her confessions, I gave her my own. She took the complicated web that held the Fallen and Hell in power here on Earth and sat with it for a long time until I explained how I'd become part of her life before meeting her.

"After I convinced my princely brothers that I was useless, I gave up my crown. There was no worth in my name so I chose a new one that would bring me power in ways no other demon had done before." She watched me from her side of the bed with her eyes glinting in the evening light. "I was loved. Admired. Worshiped by millions of fans for over a decade. It was more of a thrill than I'd ever gotten through my true name. But all mortal things must come to an end."

She hadn't forgiven me or accepted everything I said, but I didn't expect her to yet. I would have a lifetime to earn her deepest trust.

After hours of deep conversation broken up by questions about impossible things and contemplative silences, she finally fell asleep. She placed a wall of pillows between us, and I allowed her the small show of power. Her soul belonged to me, and though she was angry now, her body would not deny the connection we shared for long.

Sleep didn't find her easily. More than once she'd woken up from a nightmare of the terror she'd lived through. I'd finally had enough when she woke up screaming my name and begging for me to not leave her. I scooped her into my side and felt her melt into me. Where she belonged.

When she settled, I watched headlights dance across the ceiling for hours and listened to her breathe. The sound of her heart beating in her chest soothed the final aches of my body while it mended during the darkest hours of the night.

I'd almost lost her in the church and again when we'd gotten to safety. The wall she'd built around herself was just as impenetrable as the book she'd kept between us. In the end, something I said garnered a small crack and such a small gesture had ensorcelled me fully.

Her hand on my stomach twitched and then clung to my shirt. I couldn't remember the last time I'd been a comfort to any being. My existence had been filled with consumption and freedom from the ties of hearts. I could fulfill any bodily desire with ease, but to pour into someone's soul and be anything but untenable was new territory.

Pru saw something in me worth killing for. The

woman had seen me crumble and without a second thought impaled a man to save my life. Sure, she'd been a fan of Ezra St. Croix at first. I'd been as much of a conquest for her as she'd been for me the first night we met, but when her soul became mine, I'd felt the spark of something new. Claiming her in a moment of so much trust had ignited a craving that we would be condemned to for eternity.

The madness of not being able to find her was my own Hell, and walking into that church to see her in danger because of my enemy had both made me weak and enforced my reason to survive.

Her voice was salvific. The breath in her lungs was my new divinity.

I'd fought to stay. And I'd spend the rest of our days together thanking her for leading me home.

I reached down and brought her palm to my lips, then I gently rolled her onto her back. She whimpered in her shallow sleep, reaching out for my shoulders to bring me closer. Her hips adjusted and opened for me to settle between. My hard cock pressed against her center, her panties and my briefs sliding over our skin.

"Ezra . . . ," she whispered sleepily.

I lowered myself over her, framing her face with my arms. My skin tingled as she dragged her nails down my back and under my shirt. Our bodies ached to be as close as possible. I kissed her softly until she started to grind her hips, searching for what she craved. My tongue traced her perfect lips, mouthing pleas of relief.

The wantonness in her voice made my cock pulse.

I trailed my tongue over her jaw, to her neck, then pulled the collar of her T-shirt down to pull at the swell of her breast with my teeth. She gasped and arched her back, and I rocked my hips harder against her begging clit. The balls of my piercings rubbed over her nerves, and she bit her lip to quiet her moans, but I needed to hear her pleasure.

My ravenous soul demanded it as sacrifice for the world I was willing to burn down for her. For the miles of broken glass I would crawl through and the sins I would bleed to watch her come with my name on her tongue.

I pushed up her loose shirt and took her hard nipple into my mouth, rolling it between my teeth until she hissed. Then, with wide strokes, I soothed her until I was sure her nails would pierce my skin if I didn't stop.

"Fuck, Ezra."

My tongue dipped into the valley between her breasts and my hand slipped into her soaked panties. I plunged two fingers inside of her and pumped until she was writhing beneath me.

"Say my name, beautiful," I said into the heat of her skin.

"Gaap."

My heart skipped a beat.

"Oh please, Gaap. Fuck me."

My eyes rolled in ecstasy. Neither of us was prepared for what her request would unleash.

I pulled my cock out and gave it one preparatory stroke before sliding her panties aside. She was so wet for me but still gasped when I thrust deep. Her pussy clenched around me as she stretched, and my mouth watered.

My hand gripped the sheets around the halo of her hair, and I used the angle to fuck her until her knees were shaking at my waist. Each blow brought us closer to the edge of the storm building between her thighs. I could feel my own climax coming too fast, but I couldn't stop. I needed to be deeper.

I scooped my arm under her ass and tilted her into me to hit that spot I knew she needed. And as the tension became almost unbearable, she cried out my true name and her walls gripped and released around my shaft. My body convulsed, and I gritted her name through my teeth as I filled her.

Breathless, I collapsed onto her chest. She sank her fingers into my hair and held my head close to her chest. Her racing heart was my reward for serving her so thoroughly.

I was hers. She was mine.

This bed was our confessional. And in the sanctity of our pillows and down comforter, we were our own salvation.

15
PRU

The drought stricken scenery was a mix of grey, browns, and red clay between rooftops, too blue swimming pools, and smoggy air as we made our way back to L.A.

I hadn't gotten much sleep after Ezra woke up in a starved state after he had healed completely. Between whispered promises and long moments of wordless conversations, he'd devoured me, fucked me, and edged me until I was crying from relief.

I didn't know what to expect when we got back to his brother's club, but he'd warned me of their titles before we arrived. There hadn't been any word of a wounded priest in San Diego, and that worried Ezra more than he would tell me.

When we entered Sitri's office, the Prince of Lust, he had looked me over while stroking the inner thigh of the woman perched on his desk.

Two other men lounged on a large leather sofa. One eyed Sitri and his companion closely with a proud affection in his eyes so bright that I could have sworn I'd seen light coming from behind them.

"What have you brought back with you, brother?" the third man said, getting to his feet and holding out a hand to me expectantly.

I looked up at Ezra then down to the book I had been holding close to my heart for the duration of our return trip.

"It'll burn you . . . won't it?" I pulled back a step, but the handsome man only chuckled and pinched the thick book between his thumb and index finger.

"No, darling," he said, his voice silky and dark. "This book and I are well acquainted."

"How?" My voice cracked, but he only smiled.

"This is the only copy of the *Malleus Maleficarum* that I helped forge. You see this stained marking here?" He pointed to something that looked like a serpent lying on a box that rested on a bed of small, perfect circles. "The deal I made with its author was broken a century after I'd placed my sigil on its bindings. A fortuitous betrayal."

I let the book go as he pulled it from my grasp. He looked at Ezra and gave him a dip of his chin. "That is one debt paid. How will you fulfill the other with the Leviathan gone?"

"By taking back the burden I placed on Ipos and aiding him in finding the ring myself."

"Alone?" the blond man still sitting on the sofa chimed in, gruff disbelief in his tone. "And what about the Hunter?"

Ezra looked over his shoulder at him, then at the couple sitting at the desk. "I won't let my brothers shoulder my crown anymore. Alessio is as good as dead without the book, and he broke the treaty when he touched what didn't belong to him."

Their eyes all landed on me. My skin burned.

Sitri gave Ezra a crooked smile and a knowing nod. "Find something more in San Diego than the blasted book, then?"

Ezra's chest rose and there was determination in his next words. "I know my place on this plane. I'm sorry it took me so long to rediscover it, but I'll make it up to you."

Sitri stood and crossed the office to stand in front of Ezra and extended his hand to him. When Ezra took it, Sitri pulled him into a strong embrace.

"I'm proud to call you my brother. Welcome home, Prince of Sloth."

Sitri's words tightened my throat and brought a haze of tears to my eyes. Watching the two immortal men appreciate and acknowledge each other's weaknesses filled my heart to the brim until they pulled away and Sitri returned to his beautiful woman.

Ezra addressed the man watching the display across from me. "Eli, is there something in that book that could help me find what Ipos is looking for?"

Eli shrugged playfully, and his smile brightened to a mischievous grin. "And what will I get in return, my prince?"

Eli—I committed his name to memory—seemed to be a collector of very rare things, including favors.

"I'm guessing you wouldn't settle for backstage passes to a Luci in Furs reunion tour?" Ezra joked.

"That'll be the day," Eli mocked. His eyes settled on me. "What of this lovely treasure?"

"You wouldn't survive the night." Ezra wrapped his arm around my shoulders and tightly pulled me into his side, but not out of possessiveness.

Eli contemplated this for a moment. It wasn't a threat that I could sense, but there was an understanding that smoothed his dark features into another smile. "Then I suppose you'll owe me something else just as valuable in the future."

He shifted his gaze back to Ezra, who only nodded.

Eli opened the book, satisfied with the deal he'd struck, and flipped through the pages. Toward the middle of the yellowed chapters, he pulled out a small piece of paper that had been rolled up and tied with black hair.

"This should do it." Eli held it out for Ezra to take.

Ezra reached out, but his fingers hesitated. Before he could take another breath to fill him with courage, I reached up and took it myself. "We'll give it to him."

Eli's dark-brown eyes bored into me. At first, my stomach dropped because I thought I had over-stepped, but when he let out a loud laugh, I relaxed.

"Gaap, this human will be the death of you, but what a spectacular show that will be." He continued to laugh, and the other men in the room joined him.

"I hope she is," Ezra said down to me only, pulling my chin up and kissing me.

The laughter died away.

Sitri shook his head then looked at the blond man on the sofa. "Aren't we all begging for a love so deep that only death herself can sever it?"

Sitri and the blond man both fixed their attention on the woman on the desk, who rolled her eyes at their inside joke, if that was what it was.

Eli scoffed. "Yes, yes. Mutual adoration is all well and good, but you're all making me ill."

I couldn't help but smile at that.

"That spell should help Ipos find what he's looking for, and I will be calling upon you soon on what's owed to me," Eli finished and then vanished into nothingness.

Ezra said his goodbyes to the others and pressed his hand to my lower back to direct me out into the empty nightclub. It was eerily large without drunk dancers grinding their crotches together to the beat of house music.

"I have to go up to San Francisco," Ezra said as we crossed the dance floor toward the exit.

My chest deflated. "Oh."

"The bike won't be comfortable," he continued. "I'll have to drive."

I took one step back from him and held out the scroll. He gripped my wrist and pulled me into his arms, taking my lips with his and giving me a burning kiss that left me breathless.

"So, this time when you tease me while I'm driving, I'll have a back seat to fuck you in."

My heart leaped, and I bit my lip to stop myself from squealing.

"I'm already packed."

THE END

I f you enjoyed Prince of Sloth, please leave a review! The next Prince in Seven Deadly Sins is Ipos. Follow him up the coast in Prince of Pride.

Mai Tai Me Down

Mocktail

- 1 oz. Grenadine

- 1 oz. Lime Juice

- 1 oz. Orange Juice

- 1 oz. Pineapple Juice

- 2 oz. Mango Seltzer

- Over Ice

Ezra
st.Croix
Playlist

 Trust No One -
TX2

 Nameless -
Stevie Howie

 We Don't Have To Dance -
Andy Black

 Angels & Demons -
JXDN

 The Death Of Peace Of Mind
Bad Omens

Pru's Playlist

 Till Forever Falls Apart-
Ashe, Finneas

 Breathe-
Kansh

 Granite-
Sleep Token

 Devil Saint-
Luma, Yuppycult

 Bad Things-
Summer Kennedy

Acknowledgments

I could not be on this journey without my editor Caroline, and my proofreader Norma. The duo hear me say it all the time, but I hope they truly understand how special they are to me and my process. Knowing my books are in their hands makes my brain sigh in relief. Consider this my proclamation of love and devotion!

A special thanks to my Hype Team for being so supportive and making me smile every day. You're all so incredible!

Shout out to my Patreon members for helping make this dream go farther! Mandy, Brandi, Logan, Megan, and Marissa! You're all incredible and I can't put into words what your support means to me!